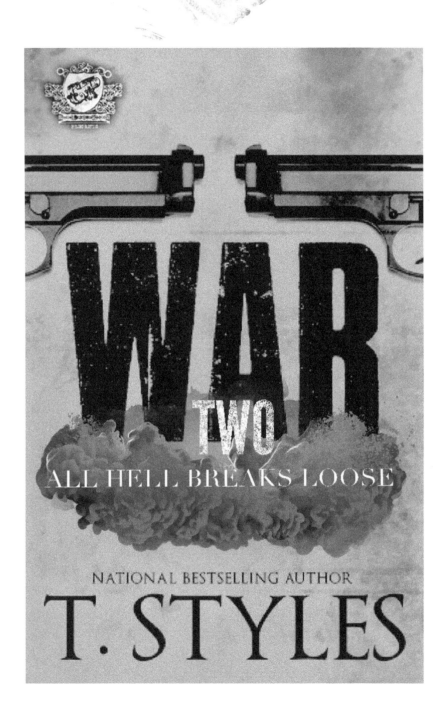

WAR
TWO
ALL HELL BREAKS LOOSE

NATIONAL BESTSELLING AUTHOR

T. STYLES

By T. Styles

ARE YOU ON OUR EMAIL LIST?
SIGN UP ON OUR WEBSITE
www.thecartelpublications.com
OR TEXT THE WORD:
CARTELBOOKS TO 22828
FOR PRIZES, CONTESTS, ETC.

4   *By T. Styles*

YOUNG & DUMB: VYCE'S GETBACK
TRANNY 911
TRANNY 911: DIXIE'S RISE
FIRST COMES LOVE, THEN COMES MURDER
LUXURY TAX
THE LYING KING
CRAZY KIND OF LOVE
SILENCE OF THE NINE
SILENCE OF THE NINE II: LET THERE BE BLOOD
SILENCE OF THE NINE III
PRISON THRONE
GOON
HOETIC JUSTICE
AND THEY CALL ME GOD
THE UNGRATEFUL BASTARDS
LIPSTICK DOM
A SCHOOL OF DOLLS
SKEEZERS
SKEEZERS 2
YOU KISSED ME NOW I OWN YOU
NEFARIOUS
REDBONE 3: THE RISE OF THE FOLD
THE FOLD
CLOWN NIGGAS
THE ONE YOU SHOULDN'T TRUST
COLD AS ICE
THE WHORE THE WIND BLEW MY WAY
SHE BRINGS THE WORST KIND
THE HOUSE THAT CRACK BUILT
THE HOUSE THAT CRACK BUILT 2: RUSSO & AMINA
THE HOUSE THAT CRACK BUILT 3: REGGIE & TAMIKA
THE HOUSE THAT CRACK BUILT 4: REGGIE & AMINA
LEVEL UP
VILLAINS: IT'S SAVAGE SEASON
GAY FOR MY BAE
WAR
WAR 2: ALL HELL BREAKS LOOSE
THE END. HOW TO WRITE A BESTSELLING NOVEL IN 30 DAYS
WWW.THECARTELPUBLICATIONS.COM

WAR 2:
ALL HELL BREAKS LOOSE

By

T. Styles

Library of Congress Control Number: 2018914160

ISBN 10: 1948373246
ISBN 13: 978-1948373241

Cover Design: Book Slut Girl

First Edition
Printed in the United States of America

What Up Fam,

I hope ya'll had a great Thanksgiving and will have a blessed Christmas. As 2018 comes to a wrap, I want to thank you all for continuing to bless my family and I with your loyalty and support. These past 10 years have been amazing and we are beyond honored that you allow us to entertain you through our stories. God bless you and all you hold dear, always.

The book in your hands is getting ready to take you on a non-stop adventure. After I picked up my jaw from reading, **"War"**, I couldn't wait to get into what was next for the Wales' and Louisville's. **"War 2"** is insane and I couldn't put it down until the last page. Cancel all your plans, this book is your new bae for the next few hours!

With that being said, keeping in line with tradition, we want to give respect to a vet or new trailblazer paving the way. In this novel, we would like to recognize:

MICHELLE OBAMA

By T. Styles

Michelle LaVaughn Robinson Obama does not need an introduction. She is Forever First Lady to Forever President Barack Obama and the first African-American First Lady. But, she's much more than that. She is a graduate of Princeton University and Harvard Law. She has just penned her memoir entitled, Becoming Michelle Obama, and it is amazing and inspiring. Make sure you add this one to your Christmas list!

Aight, I've kept you long enough...Get to it. I'll catch you in the next book.

Be Easy!

Charisse "C. Wash" Washington
Vice President
The Cartel Publications
www.thecartelpublications.com
www.facebook.com/publishercwash
Instagram: publishercwash
www.twitter.com/cartelbooks
www.facebook.com/cartelpublications
Follow us on Instagram: Cartelpublications
#CartelPublications

#UrbanFiction

#PrayForCeCe

#PrayForJuneMiller

#RIPMetha

#MichelleObama

By T. Styles

#War2

PROLOGUE
TWO DAYS LATER

C hlorine.

Blood.

Those were the odors that permeated Banks' nostrils as he opened the door leading into the large pool house. The moment he was inside, and saw what lie before him, he gasped in disbelief.

Standing near the entrance his breath rose and fell in his chest as he viewed what could only be described as a massacre. Mostly dim, only light from the pool's surface, which was red due to the bloody water, shined against his face in wave like patterns.

Slowly he walked toward the blood bath and down the silver ladder leading into the pool. This would give him nightmares he was certain. The water was crimson thick and was littered with floating limbs that bobbled along like apples in a barrel.

Banks' eyes grew blurry as tears covered his vision. He was forced to deal with what he didn't want to face.

By *T. Styles*

Did these limbs belong to those he loved? Was he moving past carnage that would later represent losing his entire family?

Again.

Wiping the tears away, he moved through the floating graveyard, picking up body part after part as his mind floated back to when things first got out of hand.

He didn't want to think about the moves he made which contributed to his family's demise. But there was no denying that this was part his fault.

Taking a deep breath he went back to the moment where once again he found himself at odds with his most worthy adversary.

His best friend.

Mason Louisville.

FCI LOW – DORM ROOM PRESENT DAY – CHRISTMAS EVE

Harris Kirk Wales' mouth was dry as he looked amongst the large group of inmates who stood around him. They were all invested in the story of why he had ordered a hit on inmate #11578, Linden Louisville, who was lying on the floor in his own blood.

Possibly dead.

No he didn't want to share his story but there he was, doing just that to a group of outlaws.

Earlier in the evening Tops, another prisoner and a larger than life presence, had ousted Kirk and his involvement with the inmate to the group. In just under an hour, all were now aware that Kirk was not who he claimed to be. Instead he was Harris Kirk Wales and the dying man was Linden Louisville—and both were members of two notorious feuding families.

Taking a deep breath, Kirk sat down on a bunk bed, preparing to talk to niggas he didn't feel he owed an explanation. And yet he was

By T. Styles

forced to do just that, as they crowded around, eager to hear more of the tale.

"So?" Byrd said waiting for him to speak. "Why you put a hit on 'em?" He asked, looking down at the inmate #11578.

"Yeah...talk, nigga," Clay added.

Kirk glared at them both for their disrespectful tongues.

Even after Tops made clear who Kirk was, the inmates were still too dumb to know where reckless yacking could get them. But if they weren't careful they were gonna find themselves in a bloody way.

Kirk wiped his hand down his face. "My father tried to tell us. If nothing else he tried to warn us about the danger that was coming our way."

"Wait...don't you mean your mother?" Byrd laughed. "Since she a bitch and all."

He gathered a few chuckles from the audience but that was the end of his fame.

Within a second Kirk had hit the man so hard his tooth hung loosely from his gum line, connected only by one thin strand of skin. "What the fuck!" He stood up and took off running to the bathroom, blood droplets along the way.

"Go follow him," Tops ordered, fearing he would tell the C.O.'s about his troubles.

One of the inmates quickly complied.

While Tops sent the man to be silenced, Kirk on the other hand had plans to give it to anyone in the dorm for disrespecting Banks and the fact that he was born a woman, who lived as a man. "Anybody else got something smart to say out they face?"

Most shook their heads no.

Amused, Tops laughed.

"And you sure you wanna hear the rest?" Kirk looked in each of their eyes, and one by one they all nodded yes, especially Clay who bobbled his head so much it looked as if it would fall at his feet.

Seconds later, Byrd returned with the inmate who fetched him moments ago. He was holding bloody tissue against his gum line, and glared Kirk's way as he took his seat.

Kirk gave it back to him in kind, ready to hit him again if he felt the need.

"Like I said, my *father* tried to warn us about the hate niggas had for us on the street. All he wanted was for us to get on that plane and...and..." He took a deep breath. "...and to

16

leave Baltimore. But as you can see by my presence here with ya'll niggas, shit ain't go as planned. Then again, it never does."

CHAPTER ONE
TWO DAYS EARLIER
FRIDAY EVENING

Pulling sweet smoke into his lungs, Banks was trying to relax.

Toking a cigar, he was seated outside on his deck, behind his home. His gaze was on the moon while the twenty soldiers who outlined the perimeter of his estate focused outward. Each was eager to puncture the lung or skull of a Lou or anyone else who felt breezy enough to overstep boundaries.

When his face itched, he scratched the X shape scar on his cheek that he got many years ago. Every now and again it bothered him, mainly when he was under pressure.

Like now.

It was easy to understand the cause of his dismay. If things went as planned, in a few days, he would be in the sky and on the way to Wales Island. But he was far from a dumb man, knowing that there were many out there who intended to stop him from his goal.

By T. Styles

As he released a pillow of smoke into the air, Bet walked outside wearing a one-piece black cat suit, which framed her body like a Picasso painting. "I still can't reach my parents." She said standing in front of him. "I'm concerned."

"Don't worry," he paused. "I'm sure they're fine."

"I hope so." She took a deep breath. "You ready?"

He looked up at her beautiful face but remained silent.

Fearful he was breaking down she sat on his lap. "It's like pulling a Band-Aid off a wound, Banks." She touched the side of his face with red manicured nails. "Once it's done it's over."

He nodded.

"Banks, talk to me." She paused. "You know I hate when I can't hear your voice."

He sighed deeply, smashed the cigar into the grey marble ground and rubbed her thigh. "You don't understand how it feels to...to feel like you gotta justify who you are, when you know what's in your heart. You don't think if I could be what they wanted me to be I would?" He paused. "But I am who I am."

"I understand but—"

"But you don't though." He paused. "Nobody does."

"I'm sorry."

He sighed deeply. "What if they...what if..."

"They will love you no matter what, Banks. We raised them right. Give them a chance to decide. I think you'll be surprised."

As much as he hated the truth he knew she was right. Despite the fact that Spacey had not taken the news of him being female well, Harris, Joey and Minnie deserved a chance.

So he nodded and tapped her thigh once.

It was time.

"Let's go," he said.

"I love you."

He winked at her and they rose.

Taking a deep breath, he smacked away the ashes that fell on his black designer t-shirt and readjusted his chain. Next he pulled up his jeans a little and looked at his wife.

Grabbing her hand, he walked into their house and into the dining room where his children awaited for the meeting. The windows were boarded up because of the gunfight so it wasn't as lavish.

But they were Wales'.

By T. Styles

Just their presence said luxury.

Sitting at the beautiful long dining room table was Banks' and Bet's children, twenty-year-old Joey, eighteen-year-old Harris and his fifteen-year-old daughter Minnesota who was referred to as Minnie.

Three trusted soldiers, who had been briefed on Banks' sexuality, hung against the wall with weapons for their protection.

"Where is Spacey?" He asked Bet.

She shrugged. "I don't know," she whispered. "Didn't wanna come I guess."

Banks nodded and took his seat. Bet sat next to him, gripping his hand so hard she slowed the blood flow through his fingertips. It was obvious she was more worried than she let on outside.

As tight as the energy was in the room, it was just as well that Spacey wasn't there. Besides, he already got a dose of what he was about to tell his siblings.

"Before I begin, I want to tell you why it was so important for me to keep you sheltered."

"We understand, Pops," Joey said. "Especially after what happened here with the shootout."

"And I forgot to tell you something about that night too, Pops," Harris added. "Something I saw from that window." He pointed at one of the boards.

"Tell me later."

"Okay, dad."

Banks ran his hand down his beard and took a deep breath. "I kept you sheltered for so long because I knew that at any point, someone would try to make a move, just to get at me. Each of you are worth millions and...if I wasn't so...so careful about who I had around you, somebody would've tried to snatch you long ago."

"Dad, what's going on?" Joey asked. "I feel you want to say something else."

"Yeah, dad," Harris said. "And why Spacey mad?"

"Spacey will be Spacey." Banks sighed. "Anyway, I have to tell you all something...something that...I mean...it may change everything." He looked down and then up at each of them.

Harris gazed at Joey and then his father. "Is this 'bout the island?" He paused. "'Cause I'm ready."

"No, son."

"Well are you okay?" Joey asked. "I mean...you not sick are you? Cause I don't think we could handle—."

Banks raised his hand. "No, son. I'm well."

They all leaned forward. "Tell us, Pops," Harris said. "We got you."

"No matter what it is," Joey added.

"Speak for yourself," Minnie said, arms crossed tightly over her 'A' cup breasts.

Her response although hurtful, was to be expected.

Her young world had recently been tilted back after learning that not only had Banks forbid her from seeing her boyfriend Arlyndo Louisville, but that she would also have to leave the country. Forever. So she wasn't in support of whatever her father was about to say.

Banks cleared his throat and looked down into his lap. "I was born a woman." Instead of beating around the bush, he felt it best to give it to them straight.

Minnie uncrossed her arms and leaned forward.

Harris blinked so many times his eyes dried out.

And Joey's jaw almost hit the table.

"Did you hear your father?" Bet asked.

Bet using the term '*father*' and Banks saying the words '*born a woman*' did nothing but confuse them even more.

"Dad, I'm...I don't understand," Joey smiled, although he felt as if he would pass out at any moment. "'Cause I thought you just said you were born a female."

"I did."

Minnie looked at Bet and then her brothers, before finally focusing on her father. She studied the shape of Banks' yellow face.

It was Masculine.

The smooth black hair resting against his skin.

It was Masculine.

The confident way he sat in his chair.

Masculine.

At the end of the day she saw nothing that would cause her to fathom him being a FEMALE.

"So if you get locked up you going to a women's prison?" Minnie asked.

Irritated, Bet said, "Why is that your question?"

Minnie opened and closed her mouth. "But...I—"

By T. Styles

"How is that possible?" Joey asked cutting her off.

Banks took a deep breath. Having gone through this with Spacey he had a little experience. "You understand what I'm saying, son. I know you do. You're smart enough to get it."

Minnie trembled as tears began to crawl down her face. She hadn't been hearing things. Banks was a woman. One moment she was spoiled rotten and on the way to in and everything she desired and the next she had her boyfriend ripped away and her father changed into a female.

"So you trans?" Harris asked.

Banks moved uneasily. He didn't subscribe to any box but if he had to pick a category that would be the closest. "Yes...I...I guess that's what I'm saying."

Minnie leaped up and moved for the exit.

"Minnie!" Bet yelled.

She stopped, turned around and faced her mother.

"Where are you going?"

"Away! I hate everybody! I hate you too and your stupid face!"

"One day you gonna find yourself in a situation where you need your family. I just hope for your sake you survive."

Minnie rolled her eyes and stormed out of the dining room. This time no one bothered to follow, except the soldier on her detail.

Still stunned, Joey sat back and looked down into his lap.

Harris took a deep breath and shrugged. "I 'on't even give a fuck for real, for real." He paused. "You still Pops to me."

Hearing his words took one of the many bricks lying on Banks' head away. But looking at Joey he waited for the pain he knew he was about to throw at him. In his mind, God wouldn't give him two blessings in a row.

"So...this mean you not gonna be our dad no more?" Joey asked forcing back tears.

Banks stood up and rushed over to him, sitting between both young men. "Of course I am," he said with his whole heart. "If anything it means I'll be there even more."

"Why you say that?" Joey asked, still very confused.

"Because I prayed for you," Banks said placing a hand over his chest. "Hard. And your mother

26　　　　　　*By T. Styles*

and Stretch were in a position to make it possible."

Hearing Stretch's name placed the final piece into the puzzle they wanted solved. If both of his parents were female, who helped bring them into existence? Now they had their answer...Stretch was their biological flesh and blood.

"So Stretch our dad?" Joey asked.

"No!" Banks yelled. "I am!"

Bet looked at Banks and then their children. "Stretch just..." she cleared her throat. "Helped."

"What about Minnie?" Joey asked. "Did Stretch help Minnie be born too?"

There were so many questions and Banks moved uneasily in his seat. "She is biologically mine. Your mother carried...she...I mean...yes he helped with her too but, I used my egg. And we used his...his...sperm." Banks felt like a fraud trying to explain how he was both able bodied and rich enough to participate in Minnie's birth.

Making a decision to go male was something that was in his heart. And yet unlike men, he could do what men couldn't. Remove one of his eggs to see that his flesh was made real. Now he wished he hadn't. Because if all of his kids were born the same, via Stretch and Bet, they would all feel equal.

"I get it, dad," Joey said although his heart ached. "And like Harris said, I don't care."

Banks looked into his eyes and pulled him into a masculine hug. When he released him, he did it all over with Harris.

In the end, when they separated, they accepted their father for the man who raised them and not the struggles he faced as a little girl.

But that didn't mean Banks' problems were over.

In fact, they had yet to begin.

The night's cool air whirled inside the opened terrace as Minnie lie face down in her bed crying uncontrollably. Snot soaked the pillow underneath her nose, making the case slick. And whenever she tried to rise, the room felt like it was spinning as she attempted to wrap her mind around what was going on in her life.

She needed an escape.

By T. Styles

After not being able to calm herself down, due to learning that her father was her mother, she stood up slowly. Feeling off balance, it had become obvious right away that something was wrong.

Breathing felt impacted as she attempted to grasp air.

Her chest grew heavier and she was certain she was about to die.

"Help," she said in a low voice.

Banging on her bedroom door once, it flew open and Stretch entered hurriedly with two men just as she fell. Seeing her lying on the floor he knelt down. "Minnie, are you okay?"

Her chest rose and fell heavily making it more difficult to gain oxygen.

Stretch turned and looked at one of the men. "Go get, Banks," he told Xavier.

"Bet and Banks went to run errands, remember?"

Stretch hadn't. "This time of night?"

"What we gonna do?" Xavier continued.

"Let's take her to the hospital." Stretch snaked his hands under her body and scooped her out the door.

"But we not supposed to take her out the house."

"Would you rather she die?"

Fifteen minutes later, Xavier steered the car.

Stretch in the passenger's position.

Minnie was in the backseat of a Mercedes van breathing rapidly, except this time she was faking. If she were honest, she would've said she was better minutes ago. Just being away from the Wales property helped but she wasn't about to let Stretch know. She even grabbed her purse, which included her phone, cash and credit cards.

As Minnie looked at Stretch, she couldn't get over how much he looked like her father, down to the light skin and short cropped curly hair. The two men even had smooth beards on their faces.

Wanting to keep the lie alive, she moaned a little. "I don't feel good."

With tensions high, Stretch who was in the passenger seat, reached back to gently touch her leg, begging with his eyes to calm down. Losing

By T. Styles

the boss's daughter to death wasn't an option, especially after he dropped the ball on being the father of his kids.

If only they knew that she was executing a great deceit, they would have taken her back immediately.

But it was too late.

The moment the light turned red, Minnie raised her head and sat up. She wanted to see where she was.

Praying she was better, Stretch looked back at her with hopeful eyes. "Are you okay?"

She smiled. "Not...not really. Chest still feels heavy." She placed her hand over her heart for effect; except it was on the wrong side.

"We're almost there." He said calmly. "Just breathe slowly."

She smiled and thought about what Banks said about being a woman. If Banks wasn't her father, maybe Stretch was. Had she stayed in the dining room she would've learned the complete truth. But once again, her spoiled behavior kept her out of the loop. "Are you...my..." She swallowed the lump in her throat. "Are you...are..." The words felt trapped.

"What is it, Minnie?" Stretch asked.

She felt bad for him and wiped a tear away. "Nothing. And Stretch, I'm sorry about this."

With that she bolted out the door and into the night.

By T. Styles

CHAPTER TWO

In his Trap House, Mason stood next to the door of the bedroom where his son Derrick was receiving a blood transfusion from Howard, his other son who was sitting at his side. Looking down at the custom-made gold and diamond Rolex watch that Banks bought him as a birthday present, he checked the time.

It seemed like forever and still his son had not opened his eyes. It didn't matter that it had only been days.

He wanted results now.

Taking a deep breath, he focused back on Derrick and was hopeful he would survive after the bullet to the groin, courtesy of the shootout at the Wales Mansion. But how could he be sure?

After the doctor ensured the needles were positioned correctly into the young men's arms he walked over to Mason. Taking a deep breath he said, "I normally do this at a hospital." He was irritated that his gambling habit forced him into a lifelong relationship with a drug dealer because his finances were trash.

"And?" Mason said.

"If this goes wrong—"

"You die." Mason said seriously. "If this goes wrong you die."

The doctor had prepared to go in on Mason after receiving a call in the middle of the night. But remembering he was talking to a powerful dangerous man, he swallowed a healthy dose of humility instead.

"I'm afraid it won't work."

"Then you better do what's *white*," Mason said.

"Do you mean *right*?"

Mason glared.

With his white skin a deeper shade of red he said, "I didn't mean to be disrespectful." He looked back at Howard and Derrick and then Mason. "He should be fine. At least the bullet went in and out. It's just that—"

"No hospital," Mason said. "Not right now."

"Why?"

"You really wanna know that? The more information you have the more likely you are to be killed."

The doctor wiped his hand down his face. "Well if he wakes, he needs to stay in bed. The

By T. Styles

least movement he makes the better." He paused. "I'll be outside."

The moment the door opened and the doc stepped out, Jersey walked inside, along with her sons, eighteen-year-old Patterson and sixteen-year-old Arlyndo.

They bopped over to their brother's bed while Jersey approached Mason. "How is he?"

"He's alive." For a moment Mason's mind went back to the other day, when he was at Banks' on the patio, smoking weed. He had told him that he loved the drug game more than his family. But after being forced with the possibility of losing his son, suddenly he changed his mind.

"When we gonna take him to a hospital? Laying in a trap house is not the best."

He frowned. Unlike her, there was no place in the world he felt more comfortable than the trap. Within its molded walls he could think straight. "Didn't you see what happened? Weren't you there? We at war." He paused. "You want him to go to a hospital and get killed?"

"Banks wouldn't hurt Derrick." She paused. "Unless you attack first. All he wants is to leave, Mason. Let him go."

"Banks already hurt Derrick," he responded. "Remember?"

She looked over at the bed at Derrick who was still asleep, and at Howard and Arlyndo who were listening attentively at them. "Can I talk to you?" She whispered. "In private?"

Reluctantly, Mason walked out and past the many soldiers who were in the living room and into another room off to the right. Closing the door he flopped on a twin bed he slept in from time to time and looked up at her. Hands dragged down his face in frustration.

"Don't rearrange my nerves, Jersey." He sighed. "Won't be good."

She sat next to him. "I don't wanna annoy you, Mason. And I know I usually take your lead but, there's something I wanna talk to you about."

Silence.

"I don't think it was Banks who shot at you," she continued.

He glared. "What you talking 'bout?"

"The night everything kicked off." She said breathing heavily. "The direction the first bullet came in was off." She ran her hand down her

By T. Styles

face. "And I been playing this in my mind over and over but—"

"First you wondered if I wanted to still fuck the nigga Banks and now you thinking all this shit a game?"

"Mason, did you see the look in Banks' eyes when that bullet came inside that window?" She paused. "Well I did. It was like time froze and he was shocked. And it been sitting on my heart."

Mason jumped up. "You naive." He pointed a long finger in her face. "Always been. Even with our son in the next room fighting for his life you still can't see straight."

She glared. "I'm not naive, Mason," she said in a low voice. "I play submissive in the bedroom because it's what we agreed on. But I'm far from dumb. Now my sons involved and I'm afraid." She touched his hand. "And if you would just give me a chance, just hear me out, I think I can stop us from experiencing more pain. I—"

"There ain't nothing else to talk about!" He yelled pushing her hand away. "And all I know about Banks is this...I'm not letting him get on that plane unless he in a pine box."

"Why though?"

Silence.

"And you wonder why I think you never got over him." She looked down. "Even though it's obvious he a man, you still see him as a girl. Don't you?"

"You tripping."

"You know what, do as you please."

"Always."

She shook her head. There was no use in talking to him. It was about her kids anyway. "We need to at least get Derrick home. Where it's cleaner and safer."

He nodded. "I'm working on that now."

When his phone rang he removed it from his pocket and answered. "I'm busy."

"So I got a call earlier," Linden said on the other end.

"About what?"

"They on the move," he paused. "And the princess is free."

Mason's eyes widened. "Minnie?"

"Yep. I think she trying to get at nephew." Linden laughed. "We were sitting up the block from the house by this mailbox, 'cause they got the property surrounded, and one of the men saw her bolt from a truck. He hits me and luckily I'm able to trail her from a far."

"Whatever you do, get her!" Mason yelled. "And when you do, bring her to me."

MOMENTS LATER

After losing so much blood over the last couple of days, Derrick opened his eyes, only to be surrounded by his siblings.

He smiled at them, happy to be alive. "Fuck ya'll niggas looking at?" The pain ripped through his wound but it wasn't anything he couldn't handle.

Everyone laughed, relieved that he was talking shit and beyond all breathing.

"You should be nice to me," Howard said raising his arm, which was connected to a needle that pumped his blood into his brother's veins. "I'm saving your life."

Derrick chuckled again and then moaned when he felt the pain. "Don't make me laugh...this shit hurts."

The room grew silent.

"I'm sorry, bruh," Arlyndo said, guilt weighing as heavy as a bag of fake tits.

But, he had reason to apologize. After learning that his girlfriend Minnie would be moving to Wales Island with her family, leaving him alone, he orchestrated a plan to put Banks on blast at a Wales and Lou dinner. Knowing full well that his father would never allow Banks to leave, since they made a lot of money together. The way his young mind saw it, at the very least, they would fight and Banks and his family would be forced to stay.

Surely when the smoke cleared, they would put the past behind them and he and Minnie could stay together. But there were no awards being given for Arlyndo's smarts, and as a result he greatly underestimated the bad blood between the two pedigrees. Because after he and his girl spoke on what should not have been told, all hell broke loose at the Wales estate. And in the end he was further apart from his girl and his brother took a slug to the groin.

"Don't apologize," Derrick said. "What's done is done."

The brothers all nodded although they were still mad at Arlyndo.

By T. Styles

"But look, let me rap to Howard alone." Derrick said.

Arlyndo and Patterson walked out.

When the door was closed Derrick looked over at Howard. "How bad are things?"

"The worst," Howard said, trying not to shed a tear. He loved the Wales so his feelings were jacked. "They beefing hard, bruh. Niggas in the living room loading up. I'm talking so many bullet boxes in the trash they filled up six hefty bags." He scratched his nose. "But I don't think it's gonna matter. They can't think of his weak spot."

Derrick nodded. "I need you to do something."

"More than giving you blood?"

Silence.

"I see you still don't got no sense of humor," Howard continued.

"THIS AIN'T FUNNY, NIGGA!" Derrick said through clenched teeth. "We gotta do something before shit gets worse!"

He crossed is arms over his chest. "Like what?"

"I want you to get a hold of Unc." He said, referring to Banks.

"You mean auntie?"

Derrick frowned. "Fuck you talking about?"

It was at that time he realized that when Derrick got hit, he was out and wasn't privy to the story rolling around Baltimore at the moment. Naturally he felt it his place to tell him every detail, leaving no item out.

When he was done the doctor had re-entered and removed the needles from both their arms. And still, upon hearing the news about Banks being a woman, Derrick felt sure he would almost die again.

"You gotta be fucking with me." Derrick said.

Howard grinned. "Nah...I'm dead ass."

Derrick sighed and then shrugged. He thought about how good Banks had been to him, and all the long talks they shared. Banks being a woman was something he couldn't conceive but he didn't care.

Besides, Banks took an interest in all Mason's sons and always told them to stack their paper for a rainy day. He also was there for huge life changes. Him being female in Derrick's mind didn't make him less powerful. The fact that he got away with it for so long made him more dangerous.

"I don't know what he is to tell you the truth, and for real I don't care."

"It don't bother you that he faking like a man?"

"Why should it?"

"What about Dad liking him as a kid?"

"All I know is Unc been 'aight with me." He paused. "And if I can stop this—"

"You can't!" Howard yelled. "That's the Lou's problem. We too busy digging in shit that don't got nothing to do with us. So fall the fuck back and heal yourself."

"How you gonna tell me what I can and can't do?"

"For starters look at you, nigga. You laying up in a bed."

Derrick sighed deeply. He was trying to calm down even though he felt like he could lay Howard on his ass if he was on his feet, or if his face was closer. "Listen, you don't want this. I know you think you stronger than me but you don't want this on your heart."

"What?"

"War," Derrick clarified. "Let me stop this. Hook up the meet."

Howard laughed arrogantly. He was feeling himself for a lot of reasons. For starters Derrick normally struck fear in him when he roared but after having taken a bullet, all of a sudden he looked harmless.

Like a child even.

Secondly, Howard had given so much blood that he was a little sloped in the mind and unaware that he was seconds away from getting punched in the forehead.

"I ain't worried about nothing," Howard shrugged. "If it be war let it be war."

"You saying that now…but we'll see about that when shit gets heated."

Howard stood up and stumbled a little. He was feeling lightheaded. "You know what, you talking that dumb shit." He pulled the covers up to his brother's neck. "Take a nap."

"Whatever, nigga," Derrick said.

When Howard left and the door closed, Derrick immediately went to forming his plan but in his condition it was obvious he would need help. His only question was which one of his brothers could he trust?

By T. Styles

Banks was moving a box carefully into one of his houses off the grid, when his phone rang. The cargo he was carrying was precious and he had to use extreme caution. He was in his private lab and preparing to ignore the caller when it rang once more.

Looking down at it, he put the box down and answered.

"Tell the truth." Mason said on the other end. "You ever really fuck with me?"

Banks frowned and flopped into a metal chair. He could hear the pain in his voice and it reminded Banks of the time he told Mason it was over. "You talking about grade school again?"

Silence.

Banks sighed. "The person you wanted me to be was never there."

"That ain't how I saw it though."

Banks smoothed his beard and frowned. "You been drinking?"

"Some."

Banks shook his head. Grade school Blakeslee was a long way from Banks Wales. And although he cared about Mason back in the day, it was never in the way he wanted.

"I think she cared...I mean..." Banks took a deep breath. Talking about himself as a woman was as gross as placing his face between a set of sweaty butt cheeks. Why was he even doing this? "Blakeslee didn't want to hurt you. But your relationship with her never felt right."

"But you did hurt me though." Mason paused. "And I would've accepted you as you were if—"

"Never!" Banks roared, hating the places he was allowing Mason to take him in the moment. It was after 11:00 at night and all he wanted was to get off the phone and on to business. "You would never have seen me as I see myself."

He was speaking truth.

Mason liked his women submissive like Blakeslee was when she was confused, and trying to figure out why she didn't feel like other girls. There was no way he could see her going butch, let alone full blown male like Banks Wales.

"Let her go, Mason." Banks said referring to the old him. "She ain't in me. Probably never was."

"She was when we fucked."

Silence.

"To tell you the truth, I don't even remember," Banks lied.

By T. Styles

Mason laughed and hung up.

CHAPTER THREE
SATURDAY
12:07 AM

Minnie rushed outside of the carryout when she saw her friend's silver BMW. Hopping into the passenger seat, she placed her seat belt on and braced for the ride.

Nasty Natty, nicknamed for her whorish ways, was loyal as fuck but as freaky as a baby boy who just discovered his ding-a-ling. You could add to her blemishes the fact that she drove as wild as a teenager on a hover board for the first time.

There was just no taming the girl.

Still, her many flaws didn't mean she wasn't a cutie or worth the trouble. Her dark skin was smooth and her natural curly hair was teased to perfection. No doubt...Nasty Natty was easy on the eyes.

"Heyyyyyyyyyyyyyyyy, bitchhhhhhhhh!" Nasty said lengthening her long pink tongue for an extended amount of time. "Where we going?"

"To your house."

Getting the word, Nasty slammed on the gas pedal, almost hitting a man in front of her as she

By T. Styles

moved for the highway. Minnie gripped the hand rest and door.

"Let me find out Poppa Banks letting you out the house."

Minnie frowned. "Why you say that?"

Nasty looked at her and slapped her own thigh. "Bitch, you playing right?" She zigzagged in and out of traffic. "You know Banks fine ass don't like me or my mama."

"Well I don't give a fuck what he likes for real." She tugged on her seat belt again, hoping it would lock in the event of a crash.

"Why you say that?"

"Because he don't mess with me and I don't mess with him."

"You sound crazy." She waved her off.

Minnie frowned. "You don't know my life, Natty."

"I ain't gotta know your life." She shrugged, hitting 80 in a 40. "I wish I had a father who showed up."

"Well what if he ain't my...I mean..."

Minnie was about to open the bag of secrets she was holding but couldn't bring herself to say the words. For starters uttering out loud that her father was actually her mother was too embarrassing for syllables.

"What if he ain't my what?" Natty continued. "What is it, Minnie?" She paused. "You holding back on something. Talk to me."

"Nah." Minnie said.

"Is it Arlyndo?"

"Kinda."

"Ya'll broke up again?"

"No...but...I mean..." She took a deep breath. "I'm thinking about running away with him."

"Girl, you do that shit and you stupid."

Minnie frowned. "How you figure?"

"I fucks with 'Lyndo." She shrugged and hit the gas pedal harder, just because there was room on the road. "But he ain't fit to be no full time."

"You must want me to cut you off."

"Because I speak facts?"

"Arlyndo would do anything for me."

"He'd do anything *to you* too." She paused. "Please don't leave your house fucking with no Arlyndo Lou. It'll be a mistake. All them niggas dirty anyway."

She frowned. "Who told you that?"

"Everybody knows they dusty." She paused. "I mean they all fine as fuck and got a coin or whatever but they still trifling."

"Nasty, stay in your lane and I'll stay in mines."

"Mine," Nasty said just to be annoying since her point wasn't received. "Ain't no 's' on mine. I keep telling you that."

Minnie rolled her eyes while looking out the window. Her friend could talk until her tongue dried up and fell into her lap. There was nothing nobody could do to keep her away from that man.

And that was just facts.

Linden tried his best to keep up with the girl in the BMW who had precious Wales cargo in her vehicle, but it was difficult. Whoever was in the driver's seat had a death wish and he wasn't trying to have one with her.

Still, he did his best to maintain pace, knowing that doing so would put him in an extreme position of power, which was always his plan.

By T. Styles

CHAPTER FOUR

After Banks left one of his houses, he and Bet sat in the back of a Yukon XL Denali with windows so black you couldn't tell where the paint ended and the window merged. Although it was late, with things moving quickly, he wanted to make sure the plane was gassed up and ready to go to their new home on Monday. He was determined that nothing would stand in the way of getting the Wales clan in the air.

When Bet smelled a familiar scent she looked over at him. "What is that weird aroma?"

He shook his head.

"I always smell it when you go to that house that you won't let us inside," She continued. "What are you making in there? It resembles fireworks."

"It's just a hobby of mine. Leave it at that."

She sighed deeply. "How you think things went?" Bet asked grabbing his hand. "With the kids?"

He looked at her and back out the window. "You mean besides Minnie storming out?"

"That's both our faults." She admitted. "Spoiled her too much."

He nodded. "It's hard to tell how things went but I'm not gonna focus on it."

"Well one thing is certain, the boys love you," she responded.

He nodded.

She sighed deeply. "Banks, with everything...I mean..."

"Yes."

"Yes what?" She paused. "You didn't even let me finish."

"You wanna know if I'm still confident that going to Wales Island is a good move." He looked at her. "My answer is yes."

She smiled.

He stared back out the window.

"If only Spacey could understand that you never meant to hurt him." She paused. "That we never meant to hurt them while keeping your secret..."

"Spacey is spoiled too." He sat back and looked straight ahead at Rev, his soldier who steered the car. Rev didn't know Banks was female so they were still speaking in code. "The others are too."

54 *By* T. *Styles*

She frowned. "Why you say that?"

"Me and my pops had problems but I never, I mean, I never got what he meant by wanting me to be tough until this very moment."

"Wish I could've met him."

"He had his shit with him," Banks admitted. "Did stuff without my approval but he understood that when you never had a struggle, you can't recognize a blessing." He shook his head. "I love my kids, I do, but if they think they got a choice in getting on that plane they don't know me. At all."

Bet never met his father but from what she learned over the course of their relationship, they sounded similar. "What are you saying?" She trembled a little. "You would hurt our kids?"

"I'm not fuckin' around with them, Bet. That's all I'm saying."

She released his hand. "I don't like how you sound."

He smiled.

He could care less.

"What's funny?" She asked.

"What kind of nigga you thought you married? For real. You shared my bed for over twenty years and you think I would put so much energy into an escape plan, only for it to fail? I thought of every detail...every one."

"Everybody misses something."

"Not me."

She shook her head. "So you threaten our kids?"

"They not thinking smart enough to make their own decisions. And we have zero time to coddle them."

"Well you're going to be mad at me too."

He frowned and then positioned his body to look into her eyes.

But she looked away and then scooted a few inches toward the door. He yanked her closer. "What is it, Bet?"

"I'm telling my parents."

He frowned. "Telling your parents what?"

"Goodbye." She paused. "That's why I went over there but couldn't reach 'em."

He gritted his teeth and his temples throbbed. "You really wanna try me? Do I seem like a man who can be poked?"

"Not saying that."

"You saying something." He said, nostrils flaring. "I'm not—"

By **T. Styles**

"Boss, something's up," Rev said as he drove past about twenty cars parked on the left and right side of the road. All of the men were standing outside of the vehicles, leaning against them, hands clutched in front of their bodies.

Banks leaned toward the front windshield to get a better view in the darkness. Each man was looking at them. He recognized a few faces. The goons belonged to Garret.

"What's happening?" Bet asked grabbing his arm.

He looked at her and then Rev. "Keep driving."

Two minutes later the truck was parked at the private airport he had been using for years. His plane was kept there. "You stay here," Banks said to Bet.

"Boss, you want me to come with you?"

"Nah. Watch my wife."

"Banks, no!" She said before grabbing his hand. "I'm scared."

He snatched away and walked coolly to the entrance. The moment he pulled the glass door open, he saw the red head who had been there for over twenty years sitting behind the counter. But something was off. Outside of the fact that she was still there late, she looked as if she saw a ghost. Mascara had run down her face and she was trembling.

"What's wrong?" He asked, freezing in place. He didn't take one more step. Instead he hung by the doorway.

"N...nothing," she said, her teeth chattering with each syllable. When her eyes slowly moved down toward the floor, he knew immediately someone was sitting behind the counter, out of his view.

Carefully he walked backwards and exited. Rushing to the truck he slammed the door. "Pull off!"

From a distance, he could see a group of men around his plane. They were dismantling the luxury aircraft in front of his very eyes.

His skin reddened.

His heart broke.

His escape plan destroyed.

"What's wrong?" Bet asked, staring at him.

"Mason trashed my plane."

"What?" She said.

"A fucking AMBUSH!" Banks said through clenched teeth. "FUCK!" He slammed his fist into his palm.

"Does this mean we not leaving Monday?"

"We leaving. I just gotta find another way."

RING. RING.

Dipping into his jean pocket, Banks removed his cell and answered. "What, Stretch?"

"Is everything okay at home?" Bet asked covering her mouth before Banks could find out what was happening.

"What is it, Stretch?" Banks said louder, sensing that his silence meant he had fucked up again.

"It's...Minnie...she's...sorry, Boss...but you gotta come home."

CHAPTER FIVE
1:24 AM

Inside one of the six black Porsche trucks on the way to the Louisville Estate, Mason was on edge knowing that at any moment, the Wales organization could make a hit, especially after realizing he had trashed the plane, thereby throwing a horse dick into Banks' plans to bounce, leaving the streets of Baltimore *cocaine dry*.

Inside of the truck were also Derrick, Arlyndo and Jersey.

Howard and Patterson were in another.

Once they entered the gates of their property, all the trucks parked in the driveway and Derrick was helped out and placed into a wheelchair. Although his legs worked, his wound made it painful to walk. Besides, he didn't have enough energy to hold himself up and needed the device for support.

Taking a deep breath, Arlyndo pushed him softly toward their home and through the large double doors.

The moment the Louisville clan entered the property, Howard and Patterson kicked trash out of their path on the way to their rooms.

The house was in a state of chaos.

Unlike the Wales mansion, the Lou's weren't much on cleanliness and it showed, which irritated Jersey to no end. Still, for the moment everyone was happy to be home.

Without altercation from Banks.

Exhausted, Mason and Jersey looked down at Derrick. "I'm gonna have your brothers put you in—"

"I been in bed for days, Pops," Derrick said looking up at him. "Let me be for a few minutes."

"Only for a little while," Jersey interrupted.

"I know, ma."

"I'm serious. Things are different now. We have to be smart and it starts with you getting well."

"She's right." Mason nodded. "I'm going to my office." He placed a hand on Derrick's shoulder. "Let me know if you need anything." He walked away.

Jersey touched the side of Derrick's face and left them alone too.

"Where you want me to roll you, nigga?" Arlyndo asked.

"I need to talk to you."

Arlyndo walked around and stood in front of him. "Talk then."

"In private." Derrick whispered. "Take me to the cave."

Arlyndo led him to the elevator and downstairs into their elaborate basement, which could be described as nothing short of a miniature Dave and Busters. They had every arcade game and gadget a man-child could desire. Ironically, outside of Mason's room, it was the neatest place in the house.

After rolling him in the center of the floor, Arlyndo walked in front of him and asked, "What you wanna rap about?"

"I ain't feeling the way Pops tryin' to keep you from your girl."

Arlyndo's jaw dropped as he flopped on the sofa. "For real?"

"Let's be clear, I think it was wrong that you fucked with the boss's daughter, and I took a hit for that shit too." He pointed to his lap for effect. "But this shit terrible. "You and your bitch shouldn't be kept apart because of this."

By T. Styles

Excited that finally somebody in the family had his side, he breathed deeply. "That's what I been saying, Derrick. Everybody keep calling me dumb for speaking up at dinner but she was gonna be my wife."

"Exactly!"

"And now she never gonna know."

"So what you wanna do?" Derrick said, egging him on even more.

Arlyndo scratched his head. For all his wanting to be with Minnie, he never gave serious thought on how he was going to get her back after the war was declared. "I can't do nothing." He shrugged. "Dad gonna kill Unc. And if he do she never gonna talk to me."

"Not really." He paused. "I gotta plan."

Arlyndo's eyes widened. "What?"

"Unc may be on some other shit but—"

"Unc Auntie now," he corrected him. "Just so you know."

"Stop being stupid," Derrick snapped, still not able to wrap his mind around the news on Banks. "I already know but ain't nothing about that nigga feminine."

Arlyndo thought about Banks' swag. "True."

"So I need you to call Stretch for me. Because if I'm right, I think I can get you and your girl back together."

"Wait, what's in it for you?"

"Nothing." He paused. "I just wanna see black love prevail."

By T. Styles

CHAPTER SIX

Banks stood in front of Stretch and ten of his soldiers trying to understand why his daughter was not home. After finding out that his plane was destroyed, and that she was gone, his rage had built up to a proportion not present since the day he took his own father's life.

"You wanna explain to me again, WHY MY FUCKING DAUGHTER GONE?" He roared.

Stretch swallowed the lump in his throat. "Banks, she, she was having a panic attack and—"

"THEN YOU CALL ME!" Banks said louder. "YOU DON'T WALK OUT THE HOUSE WITH MY KID WHEN YOU KNOW I'M BEEFING!"

Shocking everyone present, a single tear strolled down Stretch's face. Irritated by the act of sweetness, Banks turned around, placing one hand on top of his head and the other on his hip.

"Everybody but Stretch get the fuck out! And find my daughter! Don't come back without her!" He yelled, waving fists their way.

"Yes, Boss," each said as they happily got the fuck out of his rage path.

Slowly Banks walked over to the couch and flopped down. "Sit."

Stretch wiped his tear and complied, his body as stiff as a hood girl's gelled baby hairs. "I'm so, so sorry, man. And I know I been fucking up but—"

"If you ever present yourself like that again, in front of my men, you done."

Stretch nodded rapidly. "It's just that—"

Banks threw his hand up. "Don't speak."

Stretch blinked.

"I never got a chance to express how disappointed I was that you talked about the arrangement you had with me an my wife. But I figured it wasn't time since safety was priority. And we would do it on the island." He glared at him. "So tell me, what use are you to me now?"

Silence.

Banks tilted his head to the side. "You hear me talking?"

"Oh...yes...I...I was concerned that you were taking the kids away and—"

"THEM NOT YOUR FUCKING KIDS, NIGGA!" Banks said stabbing his fist into his palm. "THEM MY FUCKING KIDS!" He paused. "MINE!"

"I know but I didn't know you were taking me to the island and I guess I overreacted because I would never see them again. I wanted to make sure they—"

"Why do I get the impression I can't trust you no more?" Banks asked calmly.

If the truth could speak for itself earlier, this was the reason Stretch shed a single tear when the men were in the room. He realized that after working all his life to get into Banks' good graces, thereby giving his wife and his daughter a chance at a wealthy lifestyle, that now he had ruined it all.

"Banks, you can trust me. You know that."

"Do I?" Banks squinted. "'Cause all I have to show for it is you revealing to my son a secret I trusted you with, and then you losing my daughter. If you were in my shoes, what would you do to me?"

Stretch looked down. Taking a long deep breath he said, "Kill me."

Banks sat back and crossed his arms over his chest. He was right but he needed him. "Find my daughter."

Stretch nodded.

"NOW!" Banks roared.

Stretch jumped up and ran out the basement.

Banks made a few calls and a few minutes later Banks summoned his sons. Joey and Harris walked down the stairs, sitting on the sofa where Stretch was just seated. Banks leaned forward, placing his elbows on his thighs, hands clasped in front of him.

"Where Spacey?"

"He ain't coming."

Banks' nostrils flared. He was gonna have to fuck Spacey up sooner or later.

"There's been a change of plans. Your sister is gone and we won't be able to use my plane to go to our island."

Joey and Harris looked at each other and back at Banks.

"You want us to help find her, Pops?" Joey asked.

"No, what I want you to do is stay here. Both of you."

"But don't you need us?" Harris asked.

"Yeah, Pops. We good with shit like this," Joey added.

"I love you both, I do. But the last thing I want is for you to see who I can become, all because you disobeyed me." He paused. "Stay here."

By T. Styles

"Aight, dad," Joey nodded. "Of course."

"Good."

Banks stood up and walked away.

CHAPTER SEVEN
2:47 AM

Although big, the house was too loud. Everyone screamed and bopped nosily around, as if their worlds weren't coming to an extreme end. The same couldn't be said for the only woman of the house though.

She was a wreck and it showed on her face.

Jersey stood in the shower trying her best to wash away the problems in her life with soap and water, but it wasn't working. Too much was happening at once and Mason wasn't helping by not listening and respecting her as his wife.

After showering, when she stepped out and onto a cheese curl bag she angrily kicked it out the way, walked over to the toilet and flopped down on the closed seat.

Gross!

Her family was hood rich.

When Mason saved her from Christian, her ex-boyfriend who he killed many years ago, she was somewhat relieved. Her comfort level around gore, spoke to the dark things she witnessed as a child because even after Mason painted a canvas

By T. Styles

with Christian's blood, she still saw Mason as her way out. She could have lived with her foster family, and they would have accepted her back immediately, but Dragon, her foster brother, was the most evil man who ever walked planet Earth. With him around she would never feel safe so she chose to become Mason's wife instead, who used her as a sex tool that could bare children. He ended up being no better. Knowing nothing about her past, because he didn't ask questions. Only twenty years old when Mason first met her, he was in fact sleeping with a complete stranger.

But, she remained silent and submissive, knowing he preferred an obedient wife over everything else.

That was then.

Now she was tired and disgusted by how her sons treated their home. And how he treated her.

Jersey got the impression that her family would be just as comfortable living in the trap house as they were living in a mansion. Their home wouldn't even be furnished if the Wales hadn't picked out every stich of décor as a gift. Even Banks was hands on instead of Mason, and she figured it was to get Mason situated with living in his own crib, since he preferred his time at the Wales mansion.

Picking up the phone in the bathroom, she called the cleaning team she normally used to get her home together. It was almost 3:00 am but having a clean home was the only way she could focus.

Next she dried off and lotioned her body, before slipping into her pink panty set. Her hand was on the doorknob when she heard...

"SLAVVVVVEEE!" Mason yelled from the bedroom.

Although not in the mood to fuck, she was about to heed his call. Instead she wept quietly, her forehead pressed against the cool door. When she was done, she took a deep breath and pulled it open.

"Slave." Mason said, sitting on the bed beating his dick. "Get over here." Whenever he was stressed he liked to fuck whether she was in the mood or not.

Except she was different now.

Without acknowledging him, Jersey walked over to the closet.

"Slave," Mason said louder as if she didn't hear his freak whore ass moments ago. "On your knees."

Ignoring him again, she grabbed her blue jeans and a cute red top with matching high heel shoes.

Feeling dumb and horny at the same time he said, "Bitch, you hear me talking to you? Get the fuck over here!" He pointed at the unmade bed.

She looked at him once, rolled her eyes and walked out the door.

Mason was on pause.

In the years they had been together, she never, *ever,* ignored his call for sex. So what had gotten into her now?

He would soon find out.

8:33 AM

Banks knocked on Spacey's door three times but when he didn't answer, he pushed it open and walked inside without an invite. He was irritated when he saw him sitting at his computer with his back faced the door. And that he didn't come to the meeting earlier.

Banks crossed his arms over his chest. "You heard me knocking?" He pointed at the door with his thumb.

Silence.

Taking a deep breath, he walked over to him. "Spacey."

He tapped a few keys. "What?"

Banks gritted his jaw. "You coming with me." He paused. "Get up and put your shoes on."

Spacey looked up at him and rolled his eyes. "I ain't going nowhere. It's 8:00 in the morning anyway."

Banks slammed the MacBook shut, almost crushing Spacey's fingertips by inches. "Get your shoes and let's go."

"Why?"

"Because I told you too."

Spacey smirked and rose slowly.

Although Banks stood over him with his 6'2 frame, having gotten newfound information about Banks' sex, he thought he could give him a go. So Spacey walked past him, knocking his shoulder as he moved toward the door.

74   *By T. Styles*

Enraged, Banks rushed in front of him, grabbed him by his shirt collar and slammed him against the wall. Air rushed from Spacey's lungs and brushed against Banks' face, as Spacey desperately searched for his normal breathing pattern.

Seeing his son was having trouble, Banks released him. "Go put your fucking shoes on! You coming with me, nigga!" He stormed out, but came back. "And never try me again."

After making sure Joey and Harris were still in the house, fifteen minutes later they were in the back of Banks' truck being chauffeured by Rev.

Banks' eyes were concealed with a pair of black Gucci, smoke colored designer shades. Whenever things were on his mind, like at the moment, he hid his eyes, not wanting people to guess his next move.

"I don't understand why you want me to go," Spacey said, trying to feel Banks out. "I usually gotta press you to hang out."

Banks looked at him once and then out the window.

His son was comical.

The truth was he didn't trust Spacey to stay home and since his goal was to get the entire

Wales clan on a plane in a few days, he couldn't take a chance that Spacey would allow his anger to lead him out the door causing him to be on the hunt for him and Minnie at the same time.

"You not even gonna talk to me?" Spacey continued, never being able to handle Banks' silent treatment like everyone in the family.

Banks continued to look outside. "So now you wanna talk?"

"I don't care if you talk for real, for real," he lied.

Banks smirked. "Then let's not speak."

He wasn't going to be pulled into a game with his son. And he wasn't about to kiss his ass either. At the end of the day he was in charge and his family had better fall in line or risk trouble.

"You not my father you know?"

Banks laughed.

The young man was hilarious.

"Right over there," Banks said to Rev, ignoring his oldest spawn all together.

"Sure, boss."

When the car pulled up to a residential area, Banks opened the door. "Keep eyes on him, Rev."

"You know it." Rev replied before turning around and aiming a gun at Spacey.

By T. Styles

"You can't be serious!" Spacey said to himself, as Banks slammed the door shut.

Walking toward a small house in Ellicott City, Maryland, he knocked on the door while also gauging his surroundings. Although he was certain he wasn't being followed, he had to be careful.

When a ten-year-old kid finally opened the door he frowned, "Is Natalie here?" He looked around from where he stood.

"Who you?" The little boy snapped, looking up at him.

"She here or not?"

The boy turned around and yelled, "Ma!"

Twenty seconds later, a forty-year-old woman approached the door, wearing nothing but a Ravens Flacco jersey, no panties. The moment she feasted her eyes on Banks, she licked her dick-scented lips. It was time to shoot her shot but first she had to roll her son away with his nosey ass. "Get in the room," she told her son.

"But I wanted to go out—"

"Now!"

He ran away.

Finally alone, she licked her lips again, as they had dried out from her first tongue wipe.

"Hey there...didn't think you would ever show your face around—"

"Is Natty here?"

She placed her hands on her hips. "Ain't got no words for me huh? Think you can just show up asking about my Natty without being—"

"I'm trying to find my daughter. She here or not?"

Irritated, she poked her lips out and tried to slam the door shut. But Banks pushed his way inside, slapped her across the face and stormed through the house. When he was certain his daughter wasn't there, he walked up to the woman who was crying softly on the floor.

Reaching into his pocket, he grabbed three hundred dollars and allowed the bills to float on her body like weighted feathers. "If she comes home, call me first. You don't want to fuck with me." He walked out the door.

Standing on the steps, he made a few calls.

CHAPTER EIGHT

The sun shined bright.

And Minnie was hopeful that things would go her way.

As she leaned against Natty's BMW, in West Baltimore, talking to her brother on the phone, she wondered when she would get to see Arlyndo's face again. Her and Natty had been up at a hotel talking all night because she was waiting for Arlyndo to return her call.

He never did.

Did he break up with her? Because of the war? Her mind was mush because earlier she drank vodka, but her heart still hurt from missing him. So she was looking forward to some weed to smooth her out, which is what Natty was doing.

Originally she was going to ignore Harris' call, as she had her parents all night, but decided against it.

"I'm not coming back, Harris." She fingered her hair. "So don't ask."

"Why though?"

"Because dad...I mean..." She paused. "I don't even know what to call him no more."

"But you gotta come back."

"For what, so he can force me on that plane?"

"So what you gonna do? Live on the streets?"

"The only way I'm going is if he lets Arlyndo come too." She squinted when she saw Natty finally giving the weed man money. They had been waiting ten minutes for him to show up and she was starting to get nervous. "But look...my friend 'bout to come back over here. I gotta—"

"Wait."

"For what?" She frowned.

"Are you serious about what you said? If Dad lets Arlyndo come, to Wales Island, you'll get on the plane?"

"I swear to God I would." She said excitedly. "Why, you gonna ask him?"

"I can't make no promises but I'ma call you back in a few hours. But be careful out there and don't do nothing stupid. Dad say we being hunted."

"Dad don't know what he talking about. He worries too much."

"I hope so," he said.

After hanging up, she smiled at the possibility that Harris might be able to get through to her father. Feeling all alone, it felt good to have an ally in the family on her side, even if nothing materialized from it.

When she saw Natty walking over to her with the weed baggy, she smiled because in a minute all of her problems would go away.

Or so she hoped.

Linden sat in a car, on the block, a little ways from where Minnie stood with her friend. He was far enough not to be seen but close enough to follow them everywhere they went. Instead of snatching her off the street in broad daylight, he wanted to make sure he could get her without confrontation, so he decided to wait.

He even considered grabbing her from the hotel but police officers were sitting on the property all night due to possible drug activity.

When his cell phone rang he answered despite the drama he knew would come his way. "Yeah." He yawned.

"You got her yet?" Mason asked.

"No, but I still got eyes on her." He looked straight ahead at Minnie and then to his right at a redbone with an ass so fat it looked like she could've fallen backwards and bounced.

"What's taking you so fucking long?" Mason snapped.

"Hold up, what I tell you about coming at me like—"

"I'm sorry, man," Mason said taking a deep breath. "I just...I mean...I need that girl for leverage."

"You and Jersey fighting?" He looked at the redbone again and licked his lips.

"Fuck you say that for?"

"The other day you were like this when she wasn't home and you were trying to get some pussy. I figured—"

"Ain't nobody thinking about that bitch," he said. "Just bring me Minnie. Don't let her get away. I'm counting on you."

By *T. Styles*

Irritated, Linden tossed the phone in the passenger's seat but when it slid to the floor he bent down to pick it up.

POP! POP!

The moment he heard gunfire, he raised his head and almost shit the seat of his jeans when he saw Minnie being tossed into the backseat of a 1996 mustard yellow Chevrolet Caprice, kicking and screaming.

While Natty lay motionless in the middle of the street in a puddle of her own blood.

He had been out all morning looking for Minnie and nothing.

Finally he got a break.

Gazing down at himself, Stretch brushed invisible lint off his suit, took a deep breath and exited the truck. Quickly, he approached Derrick who was seated in his wheelchair with his brother Arlyndo who was holding the handlebars in the parking lot of Dunkin Donuts, as if it were a stroller.

This meeting was serious. If it went correctly, it had the potential to right the wrongs of Stretch's two major fuckups.

Crossing his arms over his chest he said, "What's this about?"

"I wanna meet with Banks," Derrick said.

Stretch looked down at him and unfolded his arms. "Is it, Minnie?"

Arlyndo frowned. "What about Minnie? She okay?" He didn't have his cell phone, since Mason snatched it, so he didn't know she had been calling.

Realizing that once again he said too much, Stretch cleared his throat. "She good. But...what is this about though?" He paused. "And should you even be out the house, Derrick?" He pointed at him.

"Nah...but I'm here anyway."

Stretch looked around and back at him. "What you wanna meet with Banks about? Because I don't have to tell you, that shit tense right now."

"My girl," Arlyndo blurted. "We feel like he making a mistake by not letting me be with her and—"

"I wanna meet with him about putting an end to the war," Derrick corrected his brother. "And I

84   By T. Styles

feel like if we talk, we can put this shit behind us."

Arlyndo frowned and looked down at Derrick. "What...I thought...I thought you were gonna talk to him about Minnie."

Derrick ignored him. "Stretch, tell Banks I wanna meet with him. Now."

"That's not a good idea."

"Why not?" Derrick frowned. "After everything we been through, he ain't got no love for Mason's kids no more? Are all Lou's off limits to the Wales? He may have been beefing with dad but we should be different."

"I'm not saying that."

"Then what you saying?" Derrick paused. "Plus I know your gun held the bullet that hit me. So you owe me."

Stretch was quite aware that he shot Derrick but he didn't expect he knew until that moment. In fact, if he knew Derrick was aware, he would have never met him alone. And definitely not without consulting Banks first.

"Give me a second." Stretch walked away while Arlyndo laid into Derrick for not putting in a good word on him and Minnie.

As they spoke in private, taking a deep breath Stretch made a call. It rang once and Banks answered. "What?"

"I'm here with Derrick and Arlyndo. They wanna meet."

"You playing?" He said excitedly.

"No, boss. I'm not."

"Bring them to me." Banks ordered. "And Stretch, don't let them get away."

CHAPTER NINE
NOON

Mason sat in the living room on the sofa with Linden, Garret and Cliff,

When Mason saw the maid inching closer, he turned around and said, "You got a problem?"

The maid remained silent.

"Well get the fuck out of here," Mason continued.

"But I—"

"Go downstairs you old bitch!" Linden snapped, as if Mason's rage needed a friend.

The woman ran downstairs baring a large bag of trash.

Mason took a deep breath and focused back on the men. "Now why couldn't you keep up with the car?" He asked Linden. "I'm not understanding."

"Shit happened so quick," Linden said. "And when the girl got shot, some niggas got in the middle of the street and blocked me so I couldn't follow them. The next thing I know the car was gone."

"You should've killed her, Linden," Cliff said. "When you had eyes on her you should've killed her." He repeated himself as if niggas didn't hear him the first time.

Linden glared. "Slow your roll, young nigga."

Cliff scratched his short dark and stank dreads. Prior to his come up six months ago, he was selling crack shavings on the block for a chicken box with Old Bay fries and a half and half.

So he had to be careful or his life would be on rewind.

"Fuck!" Mason said sitting back into the sofa. Somebody saw a Wales and trying to make a come up."

"I got a plan," Garret said rubbing his hands together.

Mason considered him for a minute. For real he didn't trust him but Garret had soldiers. And since there was no denying that Banks collected manpower like coins, and was prepared for combat, he knew he needed all hands on deck if he was going to win the battle. But there was no mistaking that the moment he could step to Garret for trying to go behind his back and make a deal with Banks, he would do just that.

"What is it?" Mason asked.

"Tell him you have her," Garret smiled sinisterly.

"Nah, man," Linden said waving his hand. "I'm not feeling it."

"Why not?" Garret frowned.

"For starters we ain't got her. So what if he wants to talk to her?" Focusing back on his brother he said, "Don't go that route, man."

"I'm not sure it's a bad idea." Mason said scratching his head. "This may put us where we need to be."

"Back to my question, what if he wants to talk to her?" Linden repeated. "What you gonna do then?"

Mason looked at Garret. "How sure are you that your men can find out who kidnapped her?"

"We know all the outlaws on the streets." Garret responded. "So I'm fairly sure."

"Fairly sure ain't good enough," Linden said.

Garret laughed. "Listen, I don't even know you for real. So I don't care what you think."

"He my brother," Mason said.

"I get that," Garret responded. "I'm just saying. In all the years me and you been doing business, I ain't meet him until now. So no disrespect, but I prefer if we keep interactions to just me and you, Mason."

"Well that ain't gonna work," Mason said. "If you wanna talk to me, you talking to my brother too."

Garret shifted a little in his seat. The last thing he wanted was to be cut off from the little coke scraps Mason had left. If he wanted to stay in the money business he had to calm down. "Okay, okay, let's start all over."

"Yeah, let's do that," Linden glared.

"If you tell Banks you got his kid, Mason, I promise that within twenty-four hours I'll know where she is. On everything."

"But what if you don't find her?" Linden asked Garret again.

"True." Cliff said. "You ain't answer the question."

Everyone sighed.

Why was he there again?

"If I don't find her then we'll see."

Linden smiled sinisterly. "Yeah, we will."

Garret shrugged. "For real the only thing you have to do, Mason, is figure out what you want from Banks."

Mason stared out into nothingness.

Since he put the world onto Banks' secret about being a woman, he never thought about what he really wanted from the ordeal. At the end of the day the friendship was damaged beyond repair so there was no turning back. And since Nidia didn't want to fuck with him on the coke connection, without a new plug he would be broke soon. So whether Banks lived or died, he was still going to be in the same position.

And then he remembered what he needed.

Above all else.

REVENGE.

"What you want?" Linden asked also.

"For him to pay. For everything him and his father did to the Lou's."

His decree was like music to Linden's ears.

"I'ma tell him I got Minnie and to turn himself over to me." Mason said with a lowered brow. "I'ma let that bitch come to me."

CHAPTER TEN
2:23 PM

Minnie gasped when she opened her eyes and realized she was in a tub full of cold water.

As she moved lightly, it splashed when she looked around the grungy bathroom that was foreign to her. Where the fuck was she?

And then there was the odor.

The aroma was a mixture of old urine, eggs and feces combined. This place was hell. The white walls were not visible and in its place was a black smudgy surface. The filthy faucet dripped with thick yellow water and the black and white tile floor was cracked and broken.

"Where...where am I?" She said to herself.

When she tried to move, she realized her limbs were completely weak, as if they were weighed down with cinderblocks. They weren't. Someone had obviously drugged her. She had to be smart and remember all of the things her parents taught her if she were ever kidnapped, if she was going to survive.

When she quieted her heavy breath, to calm her mind, she realized she could hear two voices

By T. Styles

on the outside. Since the door was closed it was difficult to understand what they were saying, but she had better try if she was going to collect clues on who they were and what they wanted from Minnesota Wales.

She was just about to attempt to pull herself out of the tub, when suddenly the door opened and a large grey and white blue nose pitbull waltzed inside. It had opened the door with its slimy nose and began licking her face with its huge scratchy tongue.

It was friendly but stank like a garbage dumpster in Brooklyn.

"Hey...hey you," she whispered trying to look around it's massive head and into the dark hallway outside. Now that the door was ajar, she was trying to see something. Anything. Wanting the dog to stop, she grabbed its face and it's breath smelled of shit. "What you doing?"

It continued to lap at her cheeks before walking over to the corner of the toilet and taking a piss.

"Gross," she said to herself.

Using all her strength, she pushed herself up and stumbled a little in the process. Her body still felt heavy but her adrenaline was pumping. Now on her feet, she moved toward the door with the dog right on her heels. But before she walked out, an older and younger woman rushed up to her.

Both women were white and looked like they did twenty in a max prison easily.

"Oh no you don't!" The older woman said grabbing her by the arm. "You ain't going nowhere." She paused. "Hit her Joanie! She moving."

Within seconds, Joanie stabbed her in the arm with a needle, which caused a warm sensation to overcome her body.

Minnie Wales was out cold again.

By T. Styles

CHAPTER ELEVEN

Stretch drove down the street with Arlyndo and Derrick sitting nervously in the backseat. He was talking on the phone, as he piloted the car on the way to the Wales Estate. His voice was barely audible and Arlyndo was glued in on his every word.

Arlyndo didn't feel right. His spirit said something was wrong.

"I don't trust this," Arlyndo whispered to Derrick. "Got a bad feeling."

"I'm the one who just got shot," Derrick said in a low voice. "And I say we fine. Just chill out."

"I'm telling you, man, something feels off."

Derrick looked at him while he continued to hold his thigh where the bullet pierced his flesh. "You wanna see your girl right? I mean, ain't that what this about?"

"But not like this." Arlyndo said.

"How else then? If you want the man's respect, you gotta tell him your intentions for his daughter. Leave out the part where you like to eat pussy though." He joked.

Arlyndo frowned. "He done already said he ain't fucking with me."

"I get all that. But you also have to realize that the man who helped raise you, won't cause you no harm."

"And how you know?" Arlyndo whispered.

"I just do. But you gotta be smart enough to tell Banks how you feel and—

"I think we should run." He whispered. "We shouldn't be consorting with the enemy. This dumb."

Derrick laughed softly and Stretch looked at them through the rearview mirror, even though he was still on the phone and didn't know what the Lou brothers were saying.

"We not running," Derrick whispered. "So relax."

"Please, man," Arlyndo begged. "I don't think we should be going to his house."

"You do what you—"

The moment he parted his lips and Stretch stopped at a light, Arlyndo pushed the truck door open and rolled out into the street. He was rattled. A passing car ran over his hand but it didn't stop him from catching wheels and running as fast as he could away from the truck.

96   *By T. Styles*

"What the fuck?" Stretch said pulling over. "Let me call you back, Ericka," he said to his wife before hanging up.

Confused, Stretch opened his door, stepped out and closed the back door that Arlyndo bolted from. Looking in the direction Arlyndo ran, he couldn't see him anywhere.

Running his hand down his face, he eased back into his seat, and put the car into drive. It was the second kid who got away from him in less than 24 hours. "You wanna tell me why your brother did that?"

Derrick shrugged. "Said he ain't feel comfortable."

"And you fine?"

"Should I be worried?"

Silence.

Fifteen minutes later Derrick was sitting in his wheelchair in the Wales foyer.

Surrounded by four men, Banks walked up to them.

"Where's Arlyndo?" Banks asked.

Stretch moved uneasily. "Got away."

This nigga was getting on Banks' nerves. With every passing minute. "Big mistake," Banks said to him, glaring.

The moment Derrick saw Banks' eyes, and heard his voice, he felt he made a bad decision by coming. Arlyndo was right. Something about his mood seemed darker, and it was as if he was looking at a different man.

Within seconds Stretch was lifted out of the chair by two men, flipped over like a baby being burped and patted down on all areas of his body. When they were sure he was unarmed, he was slammed back into the seat.

"What's this about?" Derrick asked looking up at Banks. His injury burned due to how they handled his body.

No one cared.

"It's me." Derrick pled. "You ain't gotta do this."

"I know who you are," Banks said sarcastically. "You family." Banks looked at Stretch. "Take him to the George Cayley Room." All the guestrooms in Banks' house were named after men who built airplanes around the world and pilots.

When Derrick was taken into the room, he was stripped of his chair and propped on the bed. The wheelchair was quickly removed and rolled out, making him immobile. Once the door was

By T. Styles

closed, only Stretch, Rev, Banks and Derrick remained.

Looking up at him, Derrick said, "Hey, Unc, I ain't gonna lie, you scaring me."

Banks rubbed his beard and goatee before crossing his arms over his chest.

Derrick swallowed. "Can you..." He cleared his throat when his voice went *Minnie Riperton* high. "Can you tell me why you treating me like this?"

"You wanted to see me right?"

"Yeah, it's just that...one minute I was shot and the next—"

"I didn't want that to happen. You know that right?"

Derrick felt slightly relieved that Banks was at least admitting that him being almost killed was a bad thing. "I know you didn't...I just want us to stop all this and get back to where we were."

"And where was that?"

"At peace."

Rev and Stretch laughed while Banks remained stone faced. "We never had peace, nephew." He paused. "Ever."

"But...I mean—"

"Your father send you?" Banks glared. "Is this a set up?"

Derrick frowned. "No...he doesn't know I'm here."

"Then why Arlyndo leave?"

"He was afraid that you was still mad at him about Minnie."

Banks nodded and looked at his men. "Oh yeah."

"But... you gonna hurt me or something? 'Cause now I don't feel so comfortable."

"How you sound, Nephew?" Banks said snidely. "I'ma tuck you in, make sure you good and get you up and on your feet again." He slapped Stretch on the arm with the back of his hand. "Get him a bite to eat." He said before turning to walk out.

"When can I...when can I go home?" Derrick asked in a low voice.

Banks stopped and looked at him. "Why you wanna go home?" Banks paused. "You gonna chill with me for a while. Ain't that what you came for?"

All three walked out, locking the door from the outside.

By T. Styles

CHAPTER TWELVE

Jersey rushed downstairs and up to the cleaning crew who were in the basement. "Why you down here when the living room ain't done?" She asked the three women. After paying them to clean the mansion, she was irritated when her home was still a mess and as a result, she had to call them back.

"Your husband is a mean bastard," the Elderly Maid said pointing at her. "I can tell you that."

Jersey frowned even though she heard no lies. "Did he do something?"

"You mean outside of throwing me out yesterday when I was trying to clean his mess?"

"Ma'am, slow down with your—"

"Nah, Mrs. Louisville, you slow down," she said sticking her hand out, palm in Jersey's direction. "Now I'm here to do a job." Hands gripped her own hips. "But I ain't one on being talked to any kind of way either. Now if you wanna—"

"Ma, you seen Derrick?" Howard asked jogging down the steps leading into the basement. Patterson was with him and both looked nervous.

"Seen Derrick?" She frowned. "Ain't he in his room?"

"Nah...that's why—"

"Hold up, Howard," Jersey said before focusing on the cleaning crew who were glued onto their every word. "That'll be all today." She told the women.

"I hear all that, but if you putting me out I still want my money," the Elderly Maid said. "I don't plays when it comes to my—"

"You know what," Jersey jabbed a hand into her pocket, pulled out a wad of cash and slammed it against the woman's cheek, before shoving her toward the steps. The other maids followed; scared they would be disrespected too. "See to it that they leave my fucking house, Pat."

"Okay, ma," Patterson said following the crew upstairs.

When they left, Jersey walked closer to Howard who was shocked at seeing his mother go off. Most of his life he knew her to be kind and demure but this was something different.

"Now where is Derrick?" She asked.

"I swear to God I don't know, ma. I went to his room to see if he wanted something to eat and noticed he was gone."

"How he get out without us seeing him?"

"I helped him," Arlyndo said, walking downstairs with Patterson. He had a bandage on the hand that had been rolled over by a car moments earlier.

They approached him. "What happened to your hand?"

"I think it's broke." He paused. "I called the doctor who helped Derrick and he patched me up. Said I'll need a cast though. A car rolled over it."

She sighed deeply, not really wanting to know the rest. Besides, she could no longer count the number of broken bones her sons had received over their lifetime. That's why the wheelchair was already in their home. One of the sons stayed in it once or twice a year. "Arlyndo, what you mean you helped Derrick? Did you take him out the house?"

"Yes, but—"

"Why?" Howard yelled.

Arlyndo took a step back. "Because he...I mean...first he told me he was gonna help me get back with Minnie and I—"

"Fuck that bitch!" Howard yelled shoving him backwards. "Everything we going through because of you and that slut! And you still out here sniffing behind her?"

"I wasn't trying to—"

"What's wrong with you, Arlyndo?" Jersey cried. "What is—"

"Wait a minute, ma," Patterson interrupted. "Exactly where is Derrick at again, Arlyndo?"

Everyone stood around him with baited breath.

Frustrated, Arlyndo flopped down on the sofa and they moved closer, standing over his guilt-ridden body. "At Banks' house. I mean...I think."

"You took him to the Wales'?" Howard asked.

"Yeah."

"Why?"

"Because the nigga tried to get me to go and I said no! You should have too!"

Jersey hit the floor and her sons quickly helped her to the couch where she cried harder.

"Arlyndo, please say you lying," Patterson said sitting next to him. "Please say you fucking around."

"I'm not," he sniffled. "We were...he asked me to set up a meet with Banks...so that...I mean...I thought he was gonna help me get my girl back but then I found out he wanted a meeting."

By T. Styles

"About what?" Patterson yelled.

"Peace." He wiped tears away. "He wanted to meet with him about peace."

"So why the fuck you here without Derrick then?" Howard yelled. "Tell me that!"

"Because I didn't feel right when we were in Stretch's truck. Told him to come with me and everything." He looked up at them. "But he wouldn't listen."

"So you left your brother, who just took a bullet, alone with a nigga you know trying to kill dad?" Howard asked, nostrils flaring. "Causing mama to cry and shit?" He pointed at her as if folks didn't hear her weeping.

"He wouldn't come." Arlyndo whispered.

"I'm 'bout to tell dad!" Howard hit it for the steps until his mother stopped him.

"NO!" Jersey yelled.

Howard froze, turned around and looked at her. His fists clenched in knots.

She sat up on the sofa. "Let me try something first." Snot strings rolled over her lips.

"Ma, dad gonna go berserk if he find out Banks got a hold of him."

"I know." She paused. "That's why I want you to give me some time. I got an idea."

CHAPTER THIRTEEN
3:30 PM

Bet steered her gold Mercedes Benz down the street as her husband laid into her for leaving the house without authorization. She was talking on her iPhone.

"I know what you saying but you not my father, Banks!" She yelled. "I'm a grown woman who—"

"Fuck is wrong with you?" He yelled. "Huh? Don't you get what's going on? I had to talk to you about something concerning Minnie. And when I come to your office, I find out you not even here!"

"What was it you wanted to talk—"

"Bet, come home now," he said in a low voice.

"I already told you I'm not coming back right now." She paused. "And I know you gonna be mad and probably give me the silent treatment but I don't—"

CLICK.

"Hello," she said into the handset as she pulled up into a beautiful residential area in

Upper Marlboro Maryland. "Banks?" When she looked at the iPhone she realized he hung up.

Tossing the cell into the passenger seat, she cried harder than she had since the war began. For over twenty years Bet had given her life to Banks and it wasn't always easy. Not only did she have to deal with the mood swings, courtesy of the hormone therapy he participated in, to look and feel male, but then there was also the truth of their relationship.

Banks was a woman. And Bet was heterosexual.

So in her mind there were many things wrong with their life.

After learning that the man she was so attracted to was actually a female, she questioned not only her sexuality but also her sanity. How could she be with a woman who believed he was a man and still call herself straight?

So after Banks revealed his secret in his kitchen many years ago, she left his mansion, believing she was done.

But why couldn't she get over him?

And then she had a conversation with her mother that she'd never forget. She asked her if love can trump what she believes is right, and her mother said, *"If when you go to sleep and wake up, and you can't think about anybody but that person, then you follow him to hell if you want him."*

So she did.

Except over the years things changed.

She never considered that he could be ruthless.

She was wrong.

And now that she saw his dark side, she reasoned it was too late.

After crying her eyes out, she wiped them clean and took a deep breath. She'd deal with him later.

Exiting her car she knocked on her parent's door. Bet had gone there the night before but no one answered.

She was shocked when the door opened and one of Banks soldiers appeared.

Her eyebrows rose. "What are you...what are you doing in my parents house?"

"You can't come in," he said pushing her back softly and closing the door as if she were a stranger.

By T. Styles

She stuck her Christian Louboutin in the doorway. "Fuck you mean I can't come in? This is my—."

"Banks said to tell you to go home and get ready to pack," he pointed over her head at her vehicle. "We'll take care of your parents."

"Are you crazy?" She glared. "I'm coming in my—"

"No you not," he said firmly.

"Excuse me!" She hit his arm with her Louis Vuitton purse.

He wanted to drop her because that shit hurt but instead he opened the door wider and moved closer. "Bet, I'm not allowed to hurt you but I am allowed to restrain you." He said seriously. "Now go home! Don't make me apply pressure."

Defeated, slowly she backed away from the door, her eyes on him the entire time. Banks had not only proven to be a madman, but he was also sneaky. She never thought he would hijack her parents to control her. And yet he did.

She also remembered telling him that her parents weren't answering her calls on their patio last night. The whole time he kept a calm face when he knew the deal.

Once inside her car, she quickly called him. "Banks...what are you doing to my parents?"

"Come home." He said calmly before hanging up.

Morbidly afraid, she put her car in drive and sped off. A mile up, her phone rang again. Hoping it was Banks and he would provide more info, she answered quickly. "Banks!"

"Bet, it's me. Jersey."

She sighed. "What you want? Now's a bad time."

"Banks has my son, Bet." She cried. "Please don't let him hurt him."

Banks has her son? Bet thought. *Is that what he had to talk to me about?*

Bet pulled over and parked. "What are you talking about?"

"He has Derrick." She cried. "And I'm begging you to do something. You and me both know our kids shouldn't get involved in any of this mess. It's between Banks and Mason."

Bet knew Jersey was right.

Children were off limits and she was once again stunned at the levels Banks reached to get his family on a plane. Now she was double

By T. Styles

thinking going to Wales Island because she couldn't account for his next move.

Still...he was her husband.

"Let me tell you something," Bet said softly. "If you ever call me again about my husband, I'll put a bullet in that nigga's head myself." With that she hung up and drove quickly to her house.

CHAPTER FOURTEEN

The stuffy odor of cigar smoke floated in the air. Banks and Stretch sat inside one of Banks' associate's living room, trying to convince him of the ultimate.

With over twenty years of flying experience, Banks had met many pilots in his lifetime, including, Vanguard Morton. The two men were as different from each other as Trump and Barack. Vanguard was white, wealthy and stuck in his ways.

While Banks wasn't afraid to take major risks, if the end result was worth it.

"Where is your brother?" Banks asked sitting back into the sofa after smashing his cigar out. It sizzled. "I thought he would be here too." He picked up his glass of whiskey.

"Why?" Vanguard raked his grey and black hair back with his fingertips.

"Just asking."

"He told me he'd catch up with you later," he paused. "But now, after learning that...well...you're leaving the country, I guess he won't."

By T. Styles

Banks sat the drink on the table and clasped his hands in front of him. "I know I'm springing a lot on you, but I don't have a lot of time. I need that plane. And I would love you to fly it. I'll pay you well."

Vanguard shifted in his seat. "So you are...a drug dealer?" Vanguard frowned.

"You really wanna know?" Banks lowered his brow.

Confused he had been consulting with a criminal for so many years; Vanguard rose, poured himself another drink and sat in the recliner across from Banks and Stretch. "I can't fly you anywhere in my plane. I'm sorry."

"Then I'll fly it myself."

"You've never piloted one as big as mine."

Banks sat back in the sofa and ran his hands down his face. "All I need is some time to learn the basic controls but the operation is the same. You know this."

"The answer is still no."

Banks' jaw twitched as he tried to keep his cool. "Why?"

Vanguard looked at Stretch and then Banks. How could he be so dumb? Now that he looked with a more discerning eye, it was obvious that they were dealers.

They were too crisp.

Like ironed one hundred dollar bills.

"I can't be in the company of drug dealers." He paused. "I'm a pilot for a nationwide airliner. It just wouldn't look right. I mean, I thought you were a restaurateur."

"I'm begging you, man," Banks leaned forward. "If you don't do this, I won't be able to get my family to safety. I need that plane."

"I love you, Banks, you know I do. We've taken trips all around the world but what you're asking...what you're saying, destroys everything I stand by. I have children and I, I just can't consort with drug dealers. I really am sorry."

Banks sighed deeply, grabbed the glass and finished his drink. "Okay." He placed the glass down, stood up and extended a hand to shake Vanguard's. "Tell your brother I said hello."

Vanguard rose and shook his hand. "I really am sorry, Banks."

Banks nodded as he and Stretch moved toward the door. Once inside the truck, Stretch and Banks sat in the back seat while Rev drove.

"What now?" Stretch asked.

"We fly out tomorrow."

Stretch scratched his head. Didn't Banks hear the man say no? "But how?"

"He's gonna let me use that plane." He paused. "Or he's gonna die." He shrugged. "His choice."

RING. RING. RING.

Snaking his hand into his pocket, he grabbed his cell phone. When he saw a familiar number, he frowned.

It was Mason.

He answered.

"What?" Banks asked with zero love in his heart.

"I want my son." He paused. "I know you got him. Jersey just told me."

Banks frowned. "Word?"

"Don't fuck with me."

Banks laughed.

"Tell me this, where is your daughter?" Mason continued.

Banks glared. "Just mentioning my daughter's name is a game you don't wanna play."

"You started this not me." Mason paused. "Bring me Derrick and I'll give you this bitch."

Banks got a fever when he heard him disrespect his youngest. But he knew he was trying to rattle him on purpose too.

"I got something better," he paused. "How 'bout you suck my dick instead."

Mason laughed hysterically. "Now me and you both know that'll be a problem."

"Why?" Banks glared. "Ain't like you ain't sucked one before."

Silence.

In an effort to rattle Mason's bones, Banks reached deep, to the time he caught Mason giving oral sex to his uncle as a kid.

And the jab hurt too.

"I'm gonna kill this bitch and—"

Banks hung up.

Stuffed the phone into his pocket and smiled.

CHAPTER FIFTEEN

The moment Bet entered the house; she rushed up to Banks, as he sat in his office. With wild angry fists, she slapped and punched him all over his chest and face as he accepted each blow. But hearing her screams, within seconds, two of his soldiers snatched her up and dropped her on the floor.

As calm as a windless sea, Banks sat on the edge of his desk.

"You can leave." He told his men. When they left, he looked down at her. "You done or you finished?"

"What did you do to my parents?" She screamed, standing up. "Huh? What did you do to them?"

"Sit down, Bet." He smiled.

"I wanna know what you—"

"SIT THE FUCK DOWN!" He yelled, pointing at the couch behind her.

Slowly she sat down, for the moment fearing for her life. "What's happening with my parents?"

"You think I would hurt them?"

"I don't know what's going on with you anymore, Banks!" She cried harder. "You don't talk to me! You don't tell me anything anymore." She sniffled and wiped her nose with the back of her hand. "Then I'm finding out from Spacey that Minnie's gone. What's happening to our family?"

"Why you keep asking me that?" He said softly. "You act like you want me to say something different."

"But...but..."

"First off, I'm protecting your parents from Mason. Trust me, they'll be safe with my men."

"I thought you didn't want them knowing you a dealer. And when did you send them to their house?"

"The day that I invited Mason over for dinner." He crossed his arms over his chest. "Cause I knew there was a possibility that things might change. I've known that nigga all my life. I know his moves before he does."

That was why she hadn't been able to talk to her mom and dad. "But they aren't involved in—"

"You think them not being involved gonna stop Mason? I did it because—"

"You're trying to control me!" She cried. "You're trying to control all of us."

By T. Styles

He laughed.

"What's so fucking funny?"

"You falling apart and I gotta tell you," he walked around his desk and plopped into his chair. "...I'm kinda disappointed." He clasped his hands in front of him, as if she were an insolent employee.

"Where's my daughter?"

"Minnie doesn't understand how good she has it here, so I'm making sure that changes."

She stood up and walked toward the front of the desk. "What does that mean?" Palms flat down.

"It means I'm teaching her a lesson she won't soon forget." He smiled. "One that will force her to remember who I am." He clasped his fingers in front of him.

"Banks, please don't do this. She's just a child."

"She did it to herself when she disobeyed me by leaving. I mean think about it, Bet. Everything...all of this is because she wanted to be with that idiot." He pointed at the door. "Now we forced to leave abruptly, instead of how I planned."

"What part of this is your fault, Banks?" She yelled. "Huh? Don't you take responsibility for any of it?"

He laughed. "Nah..." He ran his hand down his beard. "I gave her everything I never had as a kid and more."

"Banks..."

"I get it, you mad. And although I don't understand, I sympathize, but when we're on that island, away from all of this, you'll thank me."

"How do you know?"

"Excuse me?"

She walked toward the side of his chair. "How do you know I won't hate you instead?"

"Impossible."

"I'm seriously starting to rethink going."

He laughed again. "You still don't understand how this works do you? Bet, you don't have a choice."

"Banks—"

"Nah, fuck that!" He yelled standing up while looking down at her. "You were the one who pursued me remember?" He banged his fist in his palm. She jumped, thinking he would strike her instead. "You were the one who pushed into my life. I was minding my fucking business! And do

120   *By* *T. Styles*

you remember what I said, the day you came back and said you wanted to be with me?"

SILENCE.

"DO YOU FUCKING REMEMBER?" He yelled louder.

She wiped her tears, walked away and flopped on the sofa. "I don't care. And I don't remember."

He rushed around his desk and raised her chin. "I told you that niggas would try to kill you just because you mine. And that I had to hold you here to protect you." He pointed at the floor. "To make sure you safe."

She sobbed quietly.

"I also told you if you gonna be mine, you gotta be *all mine*. No work. No life outside of me. *Ever*. You thought that was a game?" His breath rose and fell heavily inside his chest.

"So I made a deal with the devil."

"Call it what you want. I stamped that pussy." He winked. "You mine."

She looked up at him. "What you gonna do with Derrick, Banks? Please don't hurt him."

"I'll do with him whatever I please." He walked to the door and opened it wide. Two men walked inside. "Keep your eyes on my wife. You lose her, you die."

He stormed out.

By T. Styles

CHAPTER SIXTEEN
5:48 PM

Harris walked toward a room within the guesthouse of the Wales Estate. Knocking on the door once, he looked behind himself several times, before knocking again. Within seconds the door flew open and a cute brown skin girl with red lemonade braids opened it wide.

She was Stretch's daughter.

Jumping into his arms, her legs dangled along the sides of his body as she kissed his lips rapidly. Once inside, she kicked it closed with the sole of her foot before he dropped her on the bed, next to her college books and Mac laptop.

"Fuck wrong with you?" She asked looking up at him.

He stood over top of her. "You ain't hear what's going on?"

"Nah, I mean, daddy told mama that we moving to Wales Island but—"

"He ain't say nothing else to you, Shay?"

She smiled.

Taking a deep breath, he sat next to her. "Did he tell you anything else or not?"

"No," she replied. "I mean, what's going on?" She stood up and straddled him, looking down into his eyes. "Talk to me."

"Where Stretch at?"

"Daddy's with Banks I think," she shrugged. For real all she wanted was to fuck but he was blowing her with the *Jeopardy*. "They been gone all day. And mama in the gym downstairs. Why?"

He took a deep breath. "I ain't gonna be able to fuck with you no more."

She stood up, took one step back and slapped his face. With both hands on her hips she glared down at him. "You said you wouldn't do this no more. Promised to stop breaking my heart." She cried.

"This ain't about breaking your heart!" He yelled. "We can't...I mean..."

"Fucking talk to me!"

He took a deep breath. "I found out...the other day...that you my...that your father is...I mean..."

She sat on his lap sideways. "Kirk, please tell me something." She kissed the side of his face where she just whacked him. She was the only one who called him by his middle name. "I love you."

"I can't fuck with you because you my sister."

By T. Styles

She frowned.

Then she giggled.

He was telling jokes.

He picked her up and sat her on the bed. Standing up he said, "This ain't funny. I'm all the way serious."

"My nigga, you ain't hardly my brother. I licked your dick for dinner last night" She waved her hand. "So you can go on ahead with that shit."

"Shay, I promise to God I'm not fucking around."

Slowly the smile disappeared from his face. "So my daddy fucking your mama?"

He took a deep breath. "I love you and I mean...we done." He walked out the door and could hear her crying heavily in the background.

Tops was driving Mason and Linden in Mason's Porsche truck. Tops had one hand on the steering wheel and the other on his cell phone. He was heavy in conversation.

Mason on the other hand was in the back, nursing a bottle of liquor. After every word he spoke, he washed his mouth out with whiskey. And since he had been talking a lot he was busted.

Normally he could keep things together, and by all accounts he still was, but having Derrick in Banks' custody and beefing with Jersey put him on edge. Forcing him to realize something he never considered.

That he really loved his wife.

And that he really lost his best friend.

When Tops' call was over, he placed the phone down and looked at them both.

Linden was in the passenger's seat.

"It's confirmed," Tops said. "He gonna try and use Vanguard's plane."

"Try?" Linden repeated. "He gonna give it to him or not?"

"Nothing is certain but my niggas interviewed a few of Vanguard's neighbors by holding barrels to their faces like mics." He chuckled. "To see if they remember seeing Banks. They all said yes."

Mason nodded. "He really think he getting on a plane." He drank some more. "After all this."

"I heard the plane he trying to get worth a few million," Linden said.

"Yeah, better than the one we fucked up," Tops said.

Mason looked out the window and then at the Rolex Banks bought him on his arm. He was running out of time. Taking a deep breath he said, "Take out the pilot."

"You mean kill him?" Tops asked.

Silence.

"Done," Tops rubbed his hands together. "I'll take care of it myself."

"And I need to find a way to get Derrick out," Mason ran his hand down his face and poured more whiskey down his throat. "I can't see Banks hurting him, but I can't be sure either."

"Banks got his house covered so that's gonna be tough." Linden paused. "I ain't telling you nothing you don't know already, but I'll see what I can do. Give me a few hours."

"Did Garret find out who got Minnie yet?" Mason continued.

"Still no word," Linden said.

Mason nodded and slid out. For the moment he was done with it all.

Linden took a deep breath.

"You still want to kill your brother after all is said and done?" Tops asked.

Linden sat back into the butter colored leather seat and looked ahead. "I'ma see how this pans out, but if I get any impression he on his old shit, I want you to hit his head."

CHAPTER SEVENTEEN

It was a motel room and it was the nastiest thing she'd ever seen.

Sitting on a twin bed, she was trying to figure her kidnappers out. But the chore was annoying because they talked about stupid matters and gave no clue on what they wanted from her.

Did they even request ransom?

The mother and daughter duo, that she now knew as Joanie (daughter) and Hutch (mother), sat on the edge of the other bed watching a small television set that still worked, despite the bullet hole through the center.

Using the skills Banks taught her, that she never knew would come in handy, she looked around slowly, observing all details...small and large. Her plan was to get as much information as possible and she was on her job. She even saw the words SWEETHEART INN on a stationary pad and finally knew where she was.

A trashy motel.

As they continued to look at an old episode of Martin on TVONE, she grabbed the pad and pen and stuck it under her shirt. Her plan was to get a hold of her parents and tell them where she was, if she ever got free.

After tucking the pad in her panties she said, "Can ya'll tell me what I'm doing here?"

Joanie turned around and looked at her before rolling her eyes. "You want us to put you out again, Rich Girl?" She asked, raising the needle filled with general anesthesia, the same drug the doctors gave patients for surgery.

"Nah, I just wanna—"

"Then shut the fuck—"

KNOCK. KNOCK. KNOCK.

Minnie jumped when someone banged at the door.

Did her parents find her?

Joanie turned the TV off and slammed her hand over Minnie's mouth. While Hutch walked toward the door, looking out the peephole. "They here."

"Let 'em in, mama."

Joanie grabbed Minnie by her arm and pushed her toward the door.

"Where are you taking me?" Minnie cried.

Once out the room, Minnie immediately noticed Rev, one of her father's soldiers. A smile spread across her face and she could breathe.

By T. Styles

"Ya'll gonna get it now!" She said arrogantly in only the child of a rich family could. "You fucking with the wrong one. My daddy gonna kill both you white bitches."

Joanie and Hutch laughed as they all walked to the truck.

They didn't respond, as she wanted. Something was off. "Wait...dad knows I'm here?" She asked seriously.

Rev looked at her, shook his head and opened the back door. Minnie crawled inside. Hutch got in on the right of her and Joanie on the left. When everyone was loaded, Rev drove down the street.

Confused, Minnie sat up to talk to Rev. "Can you tell me what—"

Joanie hit her in the side of the stomach, forcing her back in her seat. "Don't move!" She said pointing at her with a soiled nail. "You getting on my fucking nerves."

Now they did it! She thought.

Minnie quickly looked at Rev who eyed her from the rearview mirror. She was expecting him to unleash. After all, she was a princess. An heir to a multi-million dollar drug empire. Surely she deserved more respect than what the women were giving her.

"Rev, she just hit me!" Minnie cried. "Ain't you gonna do something?"

Rev smiled and continued to drive.

Why wasn't he responding?

Why didn't he hit her back?

At that time it became painfully obvious, that not only did he not care, but that Banks, once again, showcased the lengths he was willing to go to keep her in line.

Livid as fuck at the recollection, she was about to start hitting everyone she could reach with tight fists in the neck, until she glanced down and noticed that Hutch's phone had slid out of her pocket and rested on the seat next to Minnie's thigh.

Since they had taken her phone and dumped it in a toilet when they first snatched her, she made a quick movement by fake coughing, which allowed her to cover the phone with her ass cheek.

When she felt the phone under her leg, she smiled to herself. At that moment she vowed that things would be different.

By T. Styles

And so as she sat back quietly in her seat, she enacted sweet thoughts of revenge. That she was sure would put the Wales Empire on it's ass.

And it would all start with a pen and paper.

When Minnie walked into the basement, she saw every member of her family sitting on sofas.

They all had fear in their eyes.

What was going on?

Banks soldiers outlined the premises, and it appeared that they were taken hostage.

Also in attendance was Stretch, his wife Ericka who most called, Silent-icka because she never spoke to anyone outside of her husband and daughter. At the end of the day she despised the Wales family and everything they stood for.

Banks stood in front of them all, hands behind his back, a look of evil on his face.

The moment Bet saw her daughter enter, she got up and hugged her tightly. Holding her face in her hands she kissed her only daughter repeatedly on the cheeks. "Are you okay?" Bet looked her over. "Are you hurt?" Her relief was profound.

"No, I'm fine, mommy," she hugged her again. "I was so scared. I was so scared something would happen to me."

Bet hugged her again and when they were done, Minnie looked back at her father before walking over to him slowly. "Daddy, I'm so sorry," she hugged him tightly around his waist, weeping into his stomach. "Please forgive me." She looked up at him.

Shocked at her mood change, he looked down at her, although slightly suspicious. After all, now it was obvious that she knew that he was apart of the kidnap.

Shouldn't she be angrier?

But his vicious move, in his mind, wasn't his fault. She chose to run. And after Banks learned she was out on the streets, he put word out that anyone who brought her alive, would be paid handsomely. Within seconds of the call going out, every dopehead in Baltimore became his friend instead of his foe. Within an hour, it didn't take long for the mother and daughter duo to find her while purchasing weed. In the end Joanie and Hutch secured the bag.

By T. Styles

He looked into her eyes. "I'm sorry I had to do that to you, Minnie but—"

"You don't have to be sorry, daddy. I'm so stupid." She sniffled. "So dumb for believing I could do things on my own."

"Soon everything you fear will be a memory." He paused, combing her hair behind her ear. "Now I hope you know that I have to keep someone with you at all times. Until we can restore trust."

"I understand, daddy. I really do."

"And Natty will be okay. She's in the hospital but they stopped the bleeding." She figured Natty got shot but didn't realize it was that bad. It made her angrier. "We paying for her surgery."

"Okay," she sniffled.

Banks nodded. "Good. You need anything?"

"This gonna seem crazy but I've been craving hot dogs."

He laughed. "I'll make it happen."

As Minnie did her best to wrap her father's mind, Harris sat in the corner of the sofa grinning, believing it all to be a show.

He was right.

"Take your seat," he told her. "I have something to talk to you about."

After the chivalries were over, Banks addressed the crowd.

"A lot is going on. People we once fucked with are targeting us." He paused. "And I know it may look like I don't care about you, but it's not true. At the same time, I can't risk anything happening. Therefore I'm instituting a policy. You're on house lockdown." He looked at his men. "Take their phones."

Joanie and Hutch gave them Minnie's ruined phone earlier.

One by one he unearthed his other children's phones as they all griped.

"Banks, please don't do this," Bet begged.

"Don't do what?" He paused. "Make sure my family gets on that plane?" He laughed.

"What plane?" She said. "You don't have one remember?"

He thought she was funny. "Don't worry. I'm taking care of everything. Starting with making sure no one else leaves this house."

"Wow," Spacey said shaking his head. "Pops going too far this time." He whispered to Harris.

"Any questions?" Banks asked his family.

Silence.

By T. Styles

"Good, then I take it that my wishes will be carried out. Trust me, this is best."

He turned and walked away. His men remained.

CHAPTER EIGHTEEN
6:30 PM

Tops pulled up in an unassuming navy blue Honda Accord in front of Vanguard's house. Wearing a Postal Service Uniform, he grabbed a sealed box where a picture of Vanguard sat on top.

Once he took a good look at the photo, and had the features of his face in his memory, he stuffed the photo in the glove compartment and took the box up to the front door. Taking a deep breath, he rung the doorbell once and a man matching the photo appeared. He was wearing an apron and his hands were covered in white powder.

Tops cleared his throat. "I have a package for you, sir."

He smiled. "Please, come inside," he laughed. "I have my hands full."

Frowning, Tops walked into the house and into the kitchen, where the man was making a cake from scratch. The plan was to hand him the package do the do and bounce. But he was invited inside so naturally he had to accept the

By T. Styles

offer. From a distance he could hear children playing and he hoped, for their sake, that they would stay where they were.

After he washed his hands he walked over to Tops.

"Okay, I'll take it now."

Tops gave him the package and the moment his hands were full, Tops removed his gun and fired a bullet into his chest. Blood splattered on the refrigerator and in Tops' face and he wiped it away to see better.

But he was still breathing.

When the man dropped, he shot him again, until his cavities filled with blood.

As fast as he came he exited.

Back in the car and halfway down the road, Tops made an appointment with his tattoo artist to get his skin marked with another dot. Every time he murdered a man, he had it memorialized with period shaped spots on his arm. And since he killed again, he saw no reason for that to change.

After making his appointment, the next person he called was Mason to tell him the news. Normally he would reach out to Linden, since the relationship with Mason was still new, but he decided to hit the boss himself, in an attempt to get closer.

"It's done."

Mason sighed deeply. "Good, let's see him try to fly now."

Minnie sat in her room, on her bed, eating hotdogs with extra ketchup, on a trey. The container sat on her table and she squeezed it several times when he wasn't looking, putting huge globs in her hand. She didn't want food but it was all a part of her plan. The truth was that the only thing on her mind was Natty and Arlyndo. But what could she do?

She would've killed for a little privacy but Banks had security looking directly over her and everything she did, especially since she ran away once.

She looked up at him. "You know you don't have to stare me down right?"

Silence.

He was told not to engage, so he watched her but kept his words to himself.

"So you just gonna stand there and stare at me like I'm crazy?"

Silence.

Minnie sighed deeply. "If my father told you to jump off a bridge you would do it?"

Silence.

Rolling her eyes, Minnie stood up and walked to the bathroom within her bedroom.

"Hold up," the soldier said, "What you doing?

"Pissing," she said with an attitude.

He stepped closer.

"You got five minutes."

She rolled her eyes. "Whatever." She walked inside.

But right before she slammed the bathroom door, he pushed it open with a stiff arm. "Don't lock this door."

"Alright, dang," she said shoving it shut almost jamming his fingers.

The moment it was closed, she quickly removed her clothing, including her panties.

Completely naked, she placed the phone she took from Hutch on top of the sink. It had been against her body so long the screen was wet and foggy. Banks would kill her if he knew she had a cell but luckily for her he didn't.

Bending down, she removed a smeared plop of ketchup that she put on her belly moments earlier and smeared it on the seat of her panties instead. She wanted it to look like she had gotten her cycle, and to the naked untrained eye it did.

"THREE MINUTES!" The soldier said knocking on the door.

"Okay!"

Quickly she grabbed the phone, sat in the tub and dialed a number she had been trying all day, before her phone was taken. She hoped she would have better luck this time.

She did.

The moment she heard his voice it took her breath away. "Arlyndo," she whispered. "Oh my, god where have you been? I miss you so much! And then Natty got hurt and...I'm so mad." She was rambling everything at once. "Daddy had me kidnapped because he wanted to scare me and everything!"

"I miss you too," he said dryly.

His tone sounded off and she picked up on it. Their relationship was passionate and reckless,

By T. Styles

so what gave now? "Well how come it don't sound like you do?"

"What you want me to say?"

"What I...what you mean what I want you to say?" Tears rolled down her face. "I been calling you all day."

"Pops took my phone earlier. He just gave it back to me though." Arlyndo explained.

"So then I'm sure you saw that I called right?"

Silence.

"Arlyndo, say something!"

"What number is this you hitting me on?" He asked ignoring her question.

"Why? You wouldn't have answered?"

"Yeah."

"Then don't worry about that. I wanna see you. Don't you wanna see me?"

"Listen, now ain't the right time."

"The right time for what?" She cried softly. "I need you, Arlyndo. I need you today. My best friend hurt. You ain't answer my calls. I mean, can you meet me a few miles from my house?"

"You got a car?"

"Nah."

"So how we gonna meet?"

"I'm gonna—"

Before she could finish her sentence, the door opened in the bathroom. Since she was hidden behind the glass door, Minnie quickly turned the water on in the tub. "What you doing in here?" The soldier asked.

Putting her plan in action, she sat the phone down out of view of the soldier and got out of the tub naked. Picking her drawers up, she rushed toward him holding the red-seated panties in his direction. She may have been doing it for the ketchup but they were still nasty and stank, since she had worn them all day.

Shocked, the soldier turned around, not wanting to see the boss's underaged daughter naked. "Where your clothes?"

"I got my period okay!" She yelled. "You satisfied now?" She smashed them in the back of his head, leaving a ketchup stain on the base of his neck.

"Fuck is wrong with you?" He turned to face her and then turned around again.

"I wanted you to see I'm bleeding! Since you so busy coming in the bathroom."

"Your father said not to leave you alone."

She glared. "I wonder what he gonna say if he found out you tried to rape me."

By T. Styles

The soldier quickly turned around. Suddenly her being naked was the least of his concerns. Those were fighting words. "What you just say?"

"If you don't get out this bathroom, and out my room, I'm gonna tell him just that."

The soldier took a deep breath and opened the door. "I'm leaving the room but you got fifteen minutes." He pointed a yellow nail at her nose. "And then you can do whatever you want 'cause I'm coming in." He walked out.

Mason, Patterson, Howard and Jersey stood over Arlyndo as he waited for Minnie to return to the phone. They were seated in the basement waiting for the verdict.

"What's going on?" Mason whispered.

"She's doing something," he said. "I can hear her talking in the background though."

"Listen, son, I know you fucked up right now," he placed a palm on his shoulder. "And I can tell in your voice you don't want her to come. But she called and this is the break we need. Now they got

Derrick and you left him by himself. So I need you to help us out."

"You promise you won't hurt her?" He looked down at his cast.

Mason raised his left hand and placed his right hand over the middle of his chest, nowhere near his heart. "I won't touch a hair on her head."

Arlyndo nodded, took a deep breath and waited for Minnie to return, the moment he did he said, "Hey, bae."

"You gonna meet me?" She asked excitedly. "Because I don't have a lot of time."

"Yes."

"Good, because I miss you so much, Arlyndo. I can't be without you any longer."

Arlyndo looked up at his family. "I miss you too."

"How long will it take you?" She asked. "To meet me?"

"How long it's gonna take you to get there?"

"I gotta write a letter and then I can be at the spot in about twenty minutes. If I'm late don't leave me."

"Never."

CHAPTER NINETEEN

B anks was sitting in his office, on the phone. His head was throbbing as he struggled with learning that Vanguard's twin brother had been murdered. All because of him. He was certain that Mason had everything to do with it.

He was on his way out the door to check with his family when Rev approached the office. "Boss, Hutch and her daughter wanna meet with you," he said.

"Now ain't a good time."

"She says it's important."

He sighed. "Did you pay them for finding Minnie yet?"

"Yes, sir. It's about something else."

Banks ran his hand down his face and walked down to the basement where Hutch and her daughter sat. He arranged for them to be taken home later, when not as many of Mason's men covered the block.

So what did they want now?

"What is it?" Banks asked trying to keep his cool.

Hutch took a deep breath. "My phone."

Banks shrugged. "What about it?"

"It's gone."

Banks squinted. "When you lose it?"

Hutch swallowed the lump in her throat. "On the way over here. I think Minnie has it."

Banks' eyes widened as he turned in the opposite direction. Moving quickly toward his daughter's room, he was angered when he saw one of his men standing outside of the room instead of inside as he instructed. "What you doing out here?"

"She...she bled on herself and—"

Banks shoved him to the side and froze when he saw the balcony door opened, and sheets in knots hanging from the banister. Running around the room like a mad man, he saw black when he didn't find her anywhere.

Trudging out of the room, he walked up to Rev, snatched his gun and shot the soldier in the face, for taking his eyes off Minnie.

With blood splattered all over his light skin, Banks took a deep breath. "Get this trash out my house, Rev! And take them dumb bitches home."

Minnie looked behind her repeatedly as she dashed through the acres of woods covering the Wales Estate. After leaving the house via her terrace, she knew she couldn't walk on the street because she was certain her father's men would locate her, forcing her back at once.

But her focus was clear.

Nothing was going to stop her from being with Arlyndo Louisville.

After walking for thirty minutes, finally she reached the location where she and Arlyndo met in secret many times. It was a small dirt road off the outskirt of the Wales' land that had once been used for trailers, when the mansion was being built years ago. But since construction was over, it was mostly abandoned and led to the highway.

That is, if you knew where to go.

Minnie and Arlyndo did.

Cut up slightly from the brush, finally she appeared on the dirt patch land where Arlyndo was standing next to his car, hands in his pocket, a look of indifference on his face.

Rushing up to him, she hugged him tightly and he hugged her back using one arm as if she wasn't *bae*.

Separating from him, she looked up into his eyes and took a deep breath. "I can't believe..." she kissed him again. "...I, I can't believe I'm standing in front of you."

He smiled lightly. "Me either."

"Was it hard...I mean...was it hard getting out?"

He shrugged and opened her car door. "Get inside."

She nodded and quickly slid into the passenger's seat while looking toward the woods, to be sure no one was coming.

Arlyndo eased into the driver's seat and drove away.

"I would have been here earlier but I had to write a letter and mail it."

Silence.

"So talk to me," she said touching his leg. "What's been going on?"

He shrugged. "Outside of missing you?"

She blushed. "Yeah."

"I don't know for real," he said. "I mean, Pops been drinking a lot and, for real...I don't know what else to say."

She looked ahead as he continued to drive the unpaved road leading to the highway. "So you think they'll actually try to hurt each other. Mason and daddy?"

He gazed at her. "I don't know, you tell me."

She sighed deeply. "I can't talk to my father anymore so I don't know what's going on either." She positioned her body so that she could look at him clearer, her back was against the door. "All I know is that I wanna be with you." She touched his leg.

He jumped.

What was going on?

Why was he quiet?

Why was he stiff?

She looked at him closer, this time with a more discerning eye. "Arlyndo, what's up?"

He shrugged again and merged onto the highway. "Nothing."

"Why it seem like you acting funny?"

He looked at her and then back at the road. "You should've stayed home, bae." A single tear trailed his cheek. "You should've stayed home."

"But…but why?" Her teeth chattered.

"Just should have that's all."

She sat back and looked straight ahead. She could hear her pulse beating in her ears. Her pressure said danger but her heart said stay. "Arlyndo, what are you doing?"

"I never wanted anybody more than I wanted you." He shook his head, as tears came down harder. "I never wanted anything more than I wanted you."

"I feel the same." She said touching his leg again. "And you have me. That's why I'm here."

"It ain't about having you." He took a deep breath. "It's about bad timing."

"If I didn't come we couldn't be together. Daddy flying us out in a few days." She paused. "Maybe sooner."

He nodded and remained silent.

"Arlyndo," she continued. "You scaring me."

He looked at her, his eyes bloodshot red. It was at that time that she could tell that he had been crying hard, probably before he even picked her up.

She took a deep breath. "You going to hurt me. Aren't you?"

"Never."

152   *By T. Styles*

"Then why are you—"

"Be quiet now, Minnie," he sighed deeply. "Just be...I mean..." His voice trailed off. His sentence incomplete.

Minnie was shaking so hard she could barely sit still. Everything trembled. Her teeth. Her limbs. It was as if she were about to explode in any second.

Twenty minutes later they were in front of his house. The moment the car was parked, ten men rushed from Mason's mansion and up to the vehicle.

Frightened, Minnie rotated her head toward Arlyndo who looked away from her. "Why?" She cried as she was being yanked from the car, kicking and screaming. "Why, Arlyndo! I love you!" She was taken into the house.

And he was crushed with betrayal.

A minute later, Mason exited the house and sat in the passenger seat, leaving the door open. "How are you, son?"

He looked at him, tears running down his cheek. "Don't hurt her."

Mason touched his shoulder with a heavy hand. "Everything's gonna be okay. You showed your loyalty. That's all that matters now."

CHAPTER TWENTY

Rev pulled in front of Vanguard's house with Banks in the backseat of his truck on the phone. He wasn't focused, because once again Minnie escaped, fucking up his plans. She was his flesh and blood but as much as he loved her, his resentment was growing to levels he didn't know were possible for his child.

Why couldn't she obey him?

Why couldn't she fall in line?

"We've been looking everywhere but we don't see her," Stretch said. "We checking a few other places though."

Banks took a deep breath and wiped his hand down his face. "I can't believe this shit happening."

"You want me to go to Mason's?"

"No...he has the place covered," he paused. "Plus I don't want him knowing she's missing again. Especially if he doesn't have her yet." He sighed. "You head up things until I leave here."

"Of course."

"And Stretch, I need all of your attention on this. You understand what I'm saying?"

"I under—"

"I'm serious."

"I promise you this, there will be nothing else I do. I'm gonna bring her back home. Let me do this for you."

"I'm gonna hold you to it." Banks said. "This is your last chance."

"I'm on it."

Banks hung up.

Trying to clear his mind, he took a deep breath and pushed open the door. Within a minute he was sitting in Vanguard's living room again. "I'm sorry, Vanguard," Banks said. "I know what it's like to lose a brother. I lost my entire family."

"Not just a brother," Vanguard said. "My *twin.*" He paused. "His kids were here too. And found his body. They will forever be emotionally compromised behind this."

"I know, man."

"Does this have anything to do with you?"

Banks sat back and crossed his arms. "I can't call it." He leaned forward, his elbows on his knees. "But I want you to know, I'll take care of whoever did this. That's my word."

Vanguard stood up and wiped his hand down his face. Taking a deep breath he said, "This island, that you're going to, is there room for me and my..." he choked up and couldn't catch his breath.

Banks stood up and walked toward him...only a few feet between them. "What is it, man?"

Slowly Vanguard turned around. His pale face now beet red. "Is there room for me and my wife?"

"What are you asking me?"

"I can't stay here. I have nothing left."

Banks frowned. "But your job and—"

"The Aviation Association will never allow me to return to work like this. They'll always be worried that my mind is not on flight...that I'm not focused. I'm done."

Banks sat back down. "I don't know, man."

"Please," Vanguard said walking up to him, sitting on his right. "My brother is gone and it's just a matter of time before I'm forced to retire."

"What about your sons?"

"My youngest can come." He paused. "I mean, how many people are you taking?"

Banks sat back. "With my wife and kids it looks like about 5."

By T. Styles

He nodded. "What about your partner? Stretch I think you called him."

Silence.

Vanguard nodded feeling he was pressing his luck. "I have a Bombardier Challenger 605. I can seat twelve."

Banks looked away and back at him. "You get us there and you have a place to stay. For as long as you want."

Vanguard grabbed his hand and squeezed. "Thank you."

Banks nodded slowly.

"But are me and my…" He took a deep breath. "Will my wife and I be safe?"

Banks nodded. "Of course." He stood up and looked down at him. "But be ready Sunday night. We wanna be out no later than 3:00am Monday morning."

Vanguard nodded. "I'll let my family know."

Banks walked out, with a sly smile upon his face.

Things were finally moving his way.

Mason, in his attempt to stop him from going to Wales Island, made a *big* mistake. For starters he didn't know that Vanguard had a twin brother when he attempted to assassinate him. And secondly, the murder of Vanguard's brother did nothing but solidify Banks' plans for the future. Bringing him and Vanguard closer.

So in that way he owed him.

Now it was time for Banks to show Mason how much he really cared.

By T. Styles

CHAPTER TWENTY-ONE
7:49 PM

Ericka was sitting in her recliner, reading a book, when her daughter Shay walked in with a look of seriousness on her face. Closing the novel, she sat up straight to focus on her only child.

Stretch never wanted more.

"What's wrong?"

"Mommy, I have to ask you something and I don't want you getting mad."

She smiled. "What now?"

Shay clasped her hands in front of herself. "Is it true?"

"Is what true?"

"Is daddy, Harris' daddy too?"

Slowly the smile on Ericka's face melted. "What you talking about?"

Shay backed up. "I...I..."

Shay may have paused on snitch mode, but Ericka had plans the moment she heard the revelation. She always had her suspicions and now there was proof.

Ericka quickly rose and ran past her child, making a beeline for Bet's office.

"MAMA, NO!" Shay yelled.

She was gone.

The reason she was so angry was easy to understand. Ever since Ericka and Stretch had met Banks and Bet, she didn't trust them. Especially when Banks used her wedding as a way to solidify the bond between Banks and Mason. She knew at that moment he was about self. Then there were the secret meetings between Banks, Bet and Stretch.

It was as if Stretch loved Banks more than her.

Her heart said something was off and everybody called her crazy.

But now look.

Whenever she asked her husband what was going on, he claimed it was nothing. Now she was learning that her fears were warranted.

Banging harshly on Bet's office door, within a few seconds she opened it calmly, enraging Ericka even more.

Several soldiers who heard the commotion walked behind Ericka, preparing to handle the situation if things got out of control.

By *T. Styles*

"I have it," Bet said to the men.

"Are you sure?" one asked.

"Yes."

"Banks doesn't want you in your office, Mrs. Wales," he said. "He want's everybody downstairs where—"

"Let me worry about my husband."

"I'll have to talk to Banks," he continued. "I'm sorry."

"You do that."

The man walked away.

He would've pressed her a little harder but everyone knew in a matter of days, the Wales would be gone anyway. So most of the soldiers were getting lax in their behavior.

When they were alone Bet stepped back and allowed Ericka into her office. Sitting behind her desk, she braced herself. "What is it, Ericka?"

"Did my husband fuck you?"

Bet shook her head. "What are you talking about?"

"It's true isn't it?" She asked trembling. "Are your kids fathered by my husband? Is that why he wouldn't give me more children, even though I begged him?"

Bet sighed. She was amusing to her.

"I'm going to tell Banks!" Ericka continued.

"You spent so much time isolating yourself from me and my family, that you really put yourself in a position where you know nothing."

"I'm not isolating myself!" She yelled. "I didn't want my husband being involved in—"

"In what?" Bet yelled walking around her desk, standing directly in front of her. "The elaborate wedding we paid for? Your child going to private schools? Your salons?" She paused. "Exactly what part about *you not wanting to be involved* are you referring to?"

Ericka huffed and puffed as she stood in front of her. Could she hit her and survive? "You know what you should be asking is what I'm capable of."

Bet glared. "Is that a threat?"

"What if it is?"

"You know, the future isn't bright for you. Your husband been making a lot of mistakes. If I were you, I'd be careful. Real careful. You may say or do the wrong thing and then...BANG." She laughed. "Now get the fuck out of my face before I hurt you."

Bet shoved her out and slammed the door.

CHAPTER TWENTY-TWO

Five minutes from his house, Banks received a call from Mason. Glancing down at the screen, he decided not to answer. Besides, he knew what he was about to ask.

His plans for his son Derrick.

The trouble was Banks didn't know what he knew. Not only that, he had gone everywhere he could to find his daughter and at the end of the day his mind was on her.

So when his phone rang three more times, he decided to take the call. "What, Mason?"

"Daddy," Minnie said with a shaky voice.

The moment he heard her, Banks felt as if he'd been gut punched. He pulled over, sat up straight and gave her his undivided attention. "What are you...where are you?"

"Daddy, I'm so sorry," she cried harder. "I'm so sorry. I...I...I wanted to see Arlyndo but—"

"Minnie, why?" Banks begged. "Why would you go see that nigga when you know—"

"As you can tell by now I'm serious," Mason said intercepting the call. "Now I want you to bring Derrick to me. Personally."

"You making a big mistake."

"AM I?" Mason yelled. "How you figure?"

"All I wanna do is get my family out of here, man." Banks said with his whole heart. "I gave you enough coke to put you on your feet. Fuck is you doing this for?"

Mason sighed deeply and said, "Because you broke my..."

Silence.

"You took my son," Mason continued, clearing his throat.

"I DIDN'T TAKE YOUR SON, NIGGA!" Banks yelled. "HE WANTED TO MEET UP WITH ME!"

"It doesn't matter how it went down. You still got him."

"I expect you to let my daughter go or—"

"OR WHAT?" Mason yelled. "Huh? What you thought...you could leave the country and have shit go your way?"

"This ain't about you."

"Then who the fuck is it about? You got out the game without clearing it with me first. Without making sure me and my family would be okay."

"Are you fucking serious? I set you up for at least six months!"

By T. Styles

"I thought we was family!" Mason said in a low voice. "What about me? And my kids?" He laughed. "Oh let me back up...we don't matter do we?"

"Let her go, Mason." Banks warned.

"No."

"Then I want you to remember this call."

"Are you saying you won't bring my son?"

Banks was done.

He slammed his finger over the end button.

He had work to do, starting with calling the Elderly Maid who cleaned Mason's house earlier. Not only did she report back to Banks as much as possible over the past twenty-four hours, but she also made sure certain devices in the house were ready to go. After listening to how Jersey slammed money into her face and she was about to punch her, Banks hung up because the call got off track and he already had the information he needed.

Fifteen minutes later he was in his house, with five of his men following.

Going to the basement with urgency, he walked up to Spacey.

"Come with me." He turned to walk up the stairs. "You can stay here," he told the men.

They remained.

"Everything okay?" Spacey asked, worried about his disposition.

Banks stopped and faced him again. "Don't make me ask again."

A minute later, the two of them were in Banks' office alone. Banks, seated behind his desk, removed a remote for a hidden compartment in the floor. Inside were all of his children's phones which he confiscated earlier, so he could limit their outside interactions. Also inside were many journals that he wrote into over the years. As if it were a precious jewel, he picked up a gold composition book and placed it on his desk.

Smoothing it with his hand, he took a deep breath and opened the cover, stopping on the first page. On it was intricate instructions and details.

Looking up at Spacey he said, "Come here."

"Dad, are you okay?"

Banks' eyes were dark and filled with rage so he knew danger was near.

Standing up he said, "Come, Spacey. Now."

Slowly Spacey walked over to the desk, sat down and looked at the book. A skilled computer programmer and being familiar with code, he

By T. Styles

reviewed the first few pages and looked up at Banks. "Is this—"

"Turn the computer on." Banks stood next to him and pointed at his screen.

Spacey swallowed the lump in his throat, turned on Banks' computer and input the data from the book. A few minutes later, Banks' screen lit up with cameras, in every area inside Mason's house.

Mason made a major error.

Lazy as a two-day-old puppy, Mason allowed Banks to furnish every piece of furniture in his home. Although Banks loved Mason like a brother, furnishing his home had nothing to do with friendship. Banks thought in terms of the future, always, so this tool did wonders. No he didn't want to beef, but he knew it was a possibility.

And so, under the guise of having Mason's home laid, Banks installed cameras within every inch of the property, specifically the gold designer light switch covers on the walls. Although he had the power, he never used the surveillance equipment until that moment.

Sound was not possible but video was crisp, thanks to the cleaning crew, wiping the hidden cameras. And it was all Banks needed to see his enemy.

"Dad, what...what is this?"

Banks glared, as he gazed at the screen, which showed every room. "The beginning." He looked at his son. "Just the beginning."

Banks walked into the doorway of his bedroom where Bet was lying on her side, crying. Several small suitcases lined the side of the wall and he was hopeful, after bringing Minnie home, that they would be on their island in a matter of time.

"Bet," he said softly leaning against the doorframe.

Silence.

"She gonna be okay," he walked further into the bedroom, closing the door behind himself. "I don't want you worrying about shit you can't change."

Bet sniffled a little. "She's going to—"

"Be fine." He sat on the edge of the bed and rubbed her thigh. "We taught her how to escape, and we taught her how to fight." He paused. "Almost too well. That's how she got out the fucking house in the first place."

She giggled softly. "Over the terrace at that."

They both laughed lightly before falling into silence. "I'm sorry, Bet. For everything."

She breathed a sigh of relief upon hearing his words. Prior to that moment, she thought for certain he had changed so drastically from the man she fell in love with, that things would never be the same.

"Thank you."

"For what."

"Just...for saying that." She took a deep breath and sat up. "And I don't blame you."

He sat closer. "Why?"

"I blame myself," she looked at him. "I should've...I should've watched her when you left but I was so angry...so mad that you..." she sobbed harder. "That you wouldn't let me see my parents." She sniffled. "Oh, Banks...what if they hurt her?"

He pulled her into his arms. "Minnie gonna be fine. I got a plan."

"But what if it doesn't work?" Her nose nestled in the seat of his neck. He smelled of expensive cologne and it made her almost better.

"Look into my eyes."

"Banks—"

"Look at me."

She did.

"The only thing I want from you, if you do nothing else, is to trust me," he paused. "It's like when I tell you I got us, that I got you, you don't believe what I'm saying is true. Have I ever steered us wrong? I built you a world of your dreams. Wait until you see it."

"I don't mean to—"

"But that be fucking up my head, making me go off." He paused. "I'm telling you I got a plan and I promise I'll find our daughter."

"Do you think she went...like...do you think she went to his house?"

He knew she was there. Mason called earlier and confirmed. But he decided to keep it to himself. Besides, what good could it do her anyway? "I got some things in motion. I'ma find out."

He pulled her hand. She stood between his legs. Slowly he raised her shirt, and kissed her belly button.

Next his lips moved to her right hip.

And then her left.

Looking up at her he smiled. "Still fine as fuck."

She grinned and removed her shirt. His compliments fueled her because they were few and far between.

Usually his eyes said he approved though.

Focusing on her button, Bet popped it open and pulled down her zipper. In a helping mood he dragged his hands down her thighs until her pants were in a pile at her feet. Kicking out of them one by one, she stood in front of him, wearing only her red panties and bra.

He kissed her belly again, snaked his finger around the seat of her panties and into her pussy. Removing his finger, Bet moaned as she watched him suck her juices.

"Take 'em off," he demanded. "The bra too."

Needing to feel something outside of emotional distress, she quickly removed everything and stood before him, hoping he'd have a plan that would end in her calling his name. Besides, it had been weeks since they fucked and the sexual frustration was killing them both.

"Get on the bed," Banks directed.

Lying on the mattress face up, Banks crawled between her legs. Kissing her inner right thigh and then her left, he ran his tongue downward until he sat at the opening of her pussy. Entering her slowly with his tongue, he made circling motions until the tip ended on her glistening clit.

"Oh, my god, Banks...I..." she gripped the back of his head and maneuvered her waist so that she could get the most sensation for the rub. "You feel so...so..."

Knowing his wife was liable to smother him at any moment, because his pussy eating game was that fire, he used his signature move and within seconds he felt her trembling, indicating she was about to explode.

"Banks..." Bet moaned.

He continued to take care of business.

"Banks," she whispered again. "I wanna...I wanna feel you."

From between her legs, he looked up at her but continued to eat her pussy. Besides, she always talked shit when he went down, so he figured this was no different.

By T. Styles

"Banks, for real..."

He gazed up at her and knew she was serious when her eyes met his with passion. Slowly he crawled between her legs, pushed down his pants and prepared to enter her pussy with his stick when she said, "Don't use that."

Confused he said, "Don't use what?"

"I wanna...I wanna feel *you*."

He frowned. "That's what I was about to do when you—"

"Not the dildo, Banks," she whispered. "I wanna feel you. On me."

Mortified, he frowned and jumped out of bed. Her making such a request, which she hadn't ever done before, was like spitting in his face. After over twenty years of being in a relationship, they never once, had skin-to-skin contact without his dick.

If he had, Banks would be brought back mentally to who he was in the worst way. He wasn't a woman. He was a man trapped in a female's body and he thought she knew that already.

"Why would you ask me something like that?" He glared.

"What...I was—"

"So now that the word is out, to our kids, you think shit gonna change what we do in the bedroom?" He yelled. "You think we two dykes now?"

"I'm not saying that, Banks. I just wanna be closer to you. I want us to—"

"If you ever ask me something like that again, ever, I will kill you." He pulled his pants up and stormed out the room.

She sobbed loudly.

By T. Styles

CHAPTER TWENTY-THREE
9:06 PM

Jersey followed Mason inside their bedroom, where he flopped on the edge of the bed. He was on his second bottle of Whiskey and at his wits end. After being unsuccessful with Banks, he thought about his plans for Minnie. So he kicked off his shoes and was in no mood to hear his wife who had given him her ass to kiss earlier.

"So you wanna talk now, huh?" He poured liquor down his throat. "Earlier you wasn't trying to give me no pussy but—"

"Mason, what's going on with my son?" She had been a wreck ever since discovering Derrick was in Banks' custody.

"I don't know." He burped. "Stop asking me."

"So what's your plan?" She said louder.

"Derrick a trooper." He beat his chest once. "I made him that way."

"This gonna end badly. And I'm not gonna let nothing happen to the rest of my kids. You need to know that up front."

He laughed. "Yeah, aight." He poured more liquor down his throat.

"And why is Minnie here? Instead of letting Banks go like he wanted, you take his daughter? I mean, are you really thinking about Derrick's safety?"

"Give me some pussy and maybe we can—"

"I don't want to fuck you! And I'm tired of how you treat me! Tired of you talking down to me too."

"Talking down to you?" He sat the bottle on the table. "That's the agreement we made when I made you my wife, slut. What, you forgot?"

"So divorce me then!" She yelled. "I DON'T GIVE A FUCK NO MORE!"

She shocked him because of her tone. So slowly he walked over to her as she backed into the wall where she could move no further. "What you say to me?"

"Mason, I—"

With a closed fist, he struck her in the eye, knocking her to the floor. It was the first time he ever hit her and it brought her to her knees. Once she was below him, he got on hand and knee and pulled her by the front of her shirt. With a closed fist he hit her repeatedly in the center of the face until her flesh spread open like butter in a frying pan.

By T. Styles

When he was done, she lie unconscious in her own blood as he looked down at her. Exhausted and drunk, he could barely stand still.

"You don't...you don't divorce me!" He said pointing at her. "I...I..." Unable to finish his sentence he stumbled out of the room, leaving her out cold.

It was mostly dark.

And was the only room in the house that didn't have a camera, because Arlyndo broke the light switch many years ago by smashing his walls in anger.

So Banks had no eye in the sky in the one place he wanted to see most.

Mason sat in a metal chair across from Minnie in Arlyndo's room.

They were alone.

And she was stressed.

"You were his favorite," he said.

"*Were*?" She whispered.

He smiled.

"Banks wasn't..." He looked down at his bloody hands. The ones used to assault his wife moments earlier. "He wasn't always...I mean..."

She moved uneasily on the side of the bed.

"Uncle Mason," she cleared her throat. "How...I mean...how was he? In school?"

He smiled. "He told you kids?"

She nodded yes.

"And here I thought he would take that info to his grave."

"So, Uncle Mason," she kept saying *uncle* in the hopes that he would remember the past, and not hurt her like his eyes said he was capable of doing. "What kind of...I mean, person was he?"

"She was my first girlfriend."

Minnie looked down. Once again she was forced to realize who Banks really was in what she deemed a gross way. But this was about survival.

"Oh...was he—"

"I'm going to kill you." He paused. "You know that right? I don't want to but...I won't have a choice."

Her jaw hung.

And as if on queue, huge droplets of tears rolled from her eyes.

By T. Styles

"But w...why?"

"Because he will give me no choice," he paused. "And he has my son."

She didn't know.

"Uncle Mason, please don't—"

"Don't worry, your blood will make great art. And I'll be sure your father gets a copy."

She was confused. What was he talking about?

Suddenly the door opened.

"Dad, what you doing in here?" Arlyndo asked walking into his room. He looked at his father and then his girl.

Having said all he came to say, Mason stood up slowly and smiled sinisterly. "Nothing." He looked at Minnie and back at him. "Make sure she stays in this room."

Arlyndo and Minnie lie in bed inside his junky room.

His father and the way he spoke to her were still heavy on her mind.

Although she was wearing panties and a bra, which meant she didn't want to have sex, it didn't stop him from trying. "Please don't be mad at me," Arlyndo begged crawling up behind her, his chin on her shoulder. Warm breath against her cheek, his cast hand touching her arm.

She looked back at him and rolled her eyes, before sobbing harder.

"Don't cry, Minnie."

"How could you do this to me?" She whispered. "I trusted you. I love you and you...you broke my heart."

"I didn't know...I mean...Dad didn't say he would snatch you out my car. And what did he say to you in my room anyway? Earlier tonight?"

"Don't lie, Arlyndo." She sniffled. "You know he gonna hurt me. He said it himself."

He sat up in bed with his back against the headboard. Wearing only boxers. "He not gonna hurt you."

"How you know?" She turned around and looked up at him.

"Because he's my father and...I mean..."

"We don't have any control. They own us." She wiped tears away. "I'm finally starting to see that, maybe, maybe we shouldn't have said nothing at

180   *By T. Styles*

dinner that night." She turned back around and cried harder.

He moved back down behind her and kissed her neck. "If he tries to hurt you, I'll kill him."

"You just running your mouth."

"I'm serious. I won't let nobody come in between you and me. That goes for your father too...or whatever he is."

She frowned. "What that mean?"

"He a woman right?" He sat up again.

Her jaw dropped and she rose. "Wait. Your father told you too?"

"Everybody knows."

Her eyes widened. "Oh my god, my life is over."

He shrugged. "Why your life over? It ain't got nothing to do with you."

"Oh my god, he gonna be so sad." She said softly. "He—"

"Fuck that nigga," Arlyndo yelled. "I don't want you caring about him since he don't care about us."

She eased out of bed. "You don't understand...if he kept it secret this long, he didn't want nobody knowing. He, he—"

"Who you more concerned about?" He yelled. "Me or him?"

"You but—"

"Then stop acting different." He continued. "We gonna be—"

Suddenly there was a large BOOM and the lights went out. The sound had weight and rocked the floors. Within seconds the alarm system beeped repeatedly, indicating that the power was out.

"What's going on?" She asked.

"You stay here."

"Don't leave me!"

"Be back."

"Please don't go. He gonna kill me."

He grabbed her face with warm palms and looked into her eyes. "Nothing will happen to you. I promise."

He slipped into his grey sweatpants and white t-shirt before leaving the room.

Once Arlyndo was downstairs, he saw his brothers Patterson and Howard looking out the window by the door. The moonlight shining inside gave them a little light.

"What's going on?" He asked them.

By T. Styles

"I don't know," Howard said. "Something's up though."

"Why the lights out?" Arlyndo continued.

"Didn't I just say I don't know, nigga?" Howard repeated. "Stop asking stupid questions." He looked behind him. "Where your girl?"

"She good." He nodded. "She sleep." He lied.

"You better hope she don't escape."

Within seconds Mason came downstairs, wobbling a little. When Arlyndo looked at his hand he noticed it was bloody red. He hadn't seen it earlier when he was in his room but now he saw clearly. "Dad, where ma?"

All three of his sons looked at Mason, also noticing the blood. "She laying down somewhere." He paused. "And she need to with that mouth of hers."

Arlyndo frowned. "Why your...why your hand bloody?"

Mason pushed past him and looked out the window. "Don't look like a storm outside," he said ignoring him. "Fuck the lights out for?"

"I'm gonna check on ma," Arlyndo said before rushing away, moving into the darkness.

Mason looked at Patterson and Howard. "We should call the electric company."

They looked at him with distaste, still afraid of asking what was on their minds. Did he hurt their mother?

"I don't got the number," Howard said.

"Well go get it then," Mason snapped.

Howard nodded and walked away, before glaring at his father once more.

Patterson looked out the window again. "This don't feel right. "You don't think this about Banks do you?"

"Stop giving the nigga so much credit. He ain't do this."

"I don't know...maybe we should pack up and—"

"We not leaving our house," Mason said. "We safe here. Besides, if he did do it, just for us to leave, we could run into a set up."

As they paced the floor, a minute later, Linden pulled up in the driveway with Tops. Mason opened the door and approached them. "Any word?"

"Why the lights out?" Tops asked looking up at the chandeliers.

"A power outage or something." Mason said. "Any word?"

By T. Styles

"Whoa," Tops said waving his hand past his nose. "You went heavy on the bottle didn't you?"

"Did you check on what I asked you to or not?" Mason yelled.

Tops cleared his throat. "Yeah, but we didn't get Vanguard."

Mason frowned. "Who you hit then? When you told me you did kill him?"

"He had a twin brother," Linden said. "So he went down instead."

"Twin brother?" Mason roared. "Fuck you mean?"

"Sorry, man, but we didn't know." Tops continued. "You didn't tell me either. So when I went to his house, I hit the wrong Nig."

"Fuck!" Mason yelled. "Well can we still pull Vanguard? We need to find out where he parking his plane, before Banks get at—"

"Nah, we can't get to him," Linden said. "One of Garret's men got into a shoot out trying to get on the block earlier. Banks' soldiers are everywhere."

"Dad, what's that?" Patterson asked looking out the window.

Wanting to get a better view, Mason opened the door and in the distance he saw three sets of headlights approaching the house. "Get everybody and move downstairs."

"Why?" Linden said.

"We got a generator and the double bolted doors," Mason said. "This looks like an attack."

CHAPTER TWENTY-FOUR
MOMENTS EARLIER

Arlyndo walked into his mother's room and stood by the doorway. He didn't see her in the darkness, but he did notice a bloody handprint on the white wall. Walking further inside he said, "Ma...are you okay?"

Silence.

"Ma."

"I'm in here, son," she said softly. "The bathroom."

He walked inside and froze when he saw Jersey sitting on the toilet with soiled bloody tissue at her feet. She had her phone on for light, so it made her visible. Both eyes were blush red and her nose was massively swollen.

Rushing up to her, he dropped to his knees and observed her face. "What happened?" He touched her leg and then the side of her cheek. "Why you bleeding?"

"I'm okay, Arlyndo." Still seated, she turned the sink on and ran cold water, placing more tissue under it to wipe her nose. "Don't worry."

She dabbed her face and winced a little at the pain.

Arlyndo's temples throbbed. "Ma, did...did dad do this to you?" He glared. "Please tell me he ain't hit you like this." He was so mad he thought he would explode.

"Leave it, Arlyndo." She took a deep breath. "I'll be okay."

"But he can't be—"

"I don't want you fighting with your father." She said softly. "Do you hear me? Not over me. Protect your girl. Besides, its not like you haven't picked up on his ways too."

He stood up slowly. "Why you say that?"

"I know how you are with Minnie." She rose to her feet and turned the water off. "It's just a matter of time before you put her in line too. If she survives all of this."

"Never!" He said loudly. "I'd never do—"

"Where is, ma?" Howard asked walking into the bathroom with his cell phone flashlight. "Some dudes pulling up and—"

The moment he entered the bathroom and saw her face, Howard stopped where he stood. "I know this nigga didn't—"

By T. Styles

"Leave it, Howard." She begged. "Please don't make things worse than they already are. I can't take much more."

"Fuck that!" Howard went storming out the bathroom with Arlyndo and Jersey moving as fast as they could behind them. "He don't need to be hitting my mother like he crazy."

Within seconds they were in the basement, with Mason locking the door behind them. There was light downstairs because of the generator, so everyone could see what he'd done.

"What took you so long?" He yelled at the three. "You know some niggas rolling up!" The moment Mason turned around, Howard shoved him across the room.

"Why you hit, ma?" He shoved him again. "Fuck is wrong with you? Huh?" Mason was trying his best not to drop the boy even though he was too drunk.

"You hit Jersey in the face?" Linden asked Mason.

"She gonna need stitches," Tops added. "Her nose all the way 'cross her face."

"Pops, why you hit ma like that?" Patterson said. He felt faint seeing his mother's grill. "I'm not understanding."

"Don't worry what I do to your mother," Mason replied. "That's our business." He glared at all of them.

"Look at her fucking face!" Howard yelled pointing at her. "Her nose twice the size of her—"

"SOME NIGGAS ROLLING UP ON THE HOUSE AND YOU TALKING TO ME ABOUT—"

"STOP IT!" Jersey yelled flopping down on the sofa. She rubbed the sides of her temples. "I can't...I can't think right now. I'm worried about Derrick and...just stop the fighting."

Silence.

Howard glared at Mason again and sat on his mother's left side, while Patterson sat on her right, as if protecting her. Mason could hardly bring himself to look at her face because he hadn't realized he'd gone so far.

And at the same time, due to pride, an apology was out of the question.

"This shit crazy," Linden said looking at Jersey again.

"You ain't lying," Tops added.

When Tops and Linden sat on the sofa also, Mason looked down at all of them, trying to figure out what to say. As it stood he looked like the bad guy, which after beating the shit out of Jersey, he was.

"Did you call the electric company?" Mason asked.

"I didn't get a chance. You told me to come down here remember?"

"Let's strap up." Mason said walking to the large gun safe across the way. He removed twelve weapons and handed them two each. They had been loading guns since things first kicked off, so they were ready.

Tops sat the guns at his side. "I appreciate it but I stay strapped," he raised his shirt.

"Then you better now," Mason said. Clearing his throat he looked over at his wife and then his sons.

The guilt hit him again.

"Maybe they weren't coming here," Linden said, referring to the vans approaching the house. "And why you ain't keep men out front?"

"I got them out there fucking up Banks' plans that's why." Mason rubbed his temples.

Everyone grew as silent as possible as they looked at the ceiling waiting for the intruders' footsteps.

"I'm confused," Jersey said holding her face. "What's going—"

"Minnie!" Mason said looking around the room. He had drank so much that he made a huge mistake. "Where the fuck is Minnie?"

By T. Styles

CHAPTER TWENTY-FIVE
MOMENTS EARLIER

Fully dressed, Minnie opened the door exiting Arlyndo's bedroom. It had been fifteen minutes since Arlyndo left, and now she felt it was the perfect time to make a run, especially since the power was off and her boyfriend was occupied.

Creeping down the dark hallway, she moved carefully toward the steps leading to the living room. When she saw no one, she rushed to the front door, pulled it open and bumped into Garret and three other men behind him.

BANKS' OFFICE

Spacey rushed to Banks' office door and pulled it open. "Dad! I see her!" He yelled. "I see her!"

Hearing his name, Banks rushed into his office and up to the computer. From one of the cameras embedded in the light fixture, he could see his only daughter out front. And for the first time since he dismantled their power, he could breathe.

She was safe.

"What you gonna do now?" Spacey asked.

"The next part of my plan." He sat in a chair.

"What's that?"

MASON'S HOUSE

Standing in Mason's doorway, and looking past Garret, Minnie noticed three vans in the driveway.

"Who are you?" Garret asked glaring.

"I'm a friend of the family." She lied, walking past him, preparing to make a run for it.

"Not so fast." He grabbed her arm, slowing blood flow in her bicep. "How come I never met you before?"

"I don't know," she shrugged, snatching away from him. "Excuse me though." She walked around him again.

"I think that's Banks' daughter," one of the men whispered to Garret. "She look like one of them red niggas."

Garret smiled and yanked her full body by the waist and maintained his hold. "You hear my man?" He paused. "He says you a Wales."

"I don't know what he talking about." She shook her head rapidly from left to right. "I'm just a friend."

"I hear all that but for now, you coming with me." He took her kicking and screaming into the dark house.

BANKS' OFFICE

While looking at the computer screen, Banks and Spacey sat on edge. Seeing Minnie being yanked back into the house caused his temples to bubble.

"Fuck," Banks said to himself. He was so angry his yellow skin reddened. "She almost got away."

"I know," Spacey sighed deeply. "Now what?"

"Bring up the basement camera again," Banks continued. "Who in there?"

"Pat, Mason, Howard, Jersey and two other niggas I don't know."

Banks sighed. "They gotta bring her down there." He paused. "I took out the power and it's the only place with a generator and light."

"How you know they won't leave?" Spacey said.

"Cause they being hunted."

Spacey sat back. "I wanna ask you something, and I don't want you to get mad."

Banks glared at him. "The last time you said that I almost crashed my plane."

"This ain't that bad."

He nodded. "What is it?"

"I was talking to Harris about something Minnie told him."

"What?" Banks asked, eyes still on the cameras.

"You think, if you let Arlyndo come with us to Wales Island, that Minnie would act right?"

196

"Nah."

"Why though?"

"Cause he ain't the one."

"Even if—"

"I didn't want her with a Lou, because I know what kind of man Mason is. He ain't raising men with respect and honor. He breeds maniacs. And I want better for my daughter."

"How you meet Mason?"

Banks sat back and folded his arms over his chest. Telling his son that they dated as children was not something he was prepared to do. "Pull up all the screens and keep your eyes peeled, Space."

Spacey nodded and did as he was told. Within seconds, he squinted. "Dad, I think I see something." He pointed at the computer.

Banks looked at one of the camera angles in the hallway leading to the basement and saw a familiar face. "Is that Garret?" He said to himself.

"I think that's the one who grabbed her outside," Spacey said.

"I know, but I didn't see his face at first." Banks tapped his shoulder. "Move over."

Banks knew him well. Garret used to cop coke from Mason, but when he killed one of Garret's men, he went over Mason's head to go directly to Banks. So He didn't understand how they reconnected because Banks, hating disloyalty, let Mason know.

Spacey rolled the chair out the way so that Banks could put his in front of the screen. "Wow," Banks shook his head and glared. "This nigga stabs him in the back and they—"

"There Minnie go right there!" Spacey yelled pointing at the computer.

Banks smiled and removed his gold composition book. Next he toggled to another screen on his computer. Entering a few keys, he sat back and waited as a timer moved backwards from 120.

Spacey tried to understand what was happening but was confused. "Dad, what's that?"

Banks grabbed his cell phone and made a call. "Meet me in the foyer."

When the call was over Banks continued to focus on the screen. "Be ready, Minnie." He said to himself. "Be ready."

CHAPTER TWENTY-SIX
TWO MINUTES EARLIER

Garret walked toward the basement door using his phone for light and tried to turn the knob to enter. But the heavy steel frame would not provide him entry. So he knocked once.

"Stay armed," he told one of his men who followed. "I don't know who in there." He looked at Minnie Wales and wondered if she had made a move and killed everyone inside.

"Whoever you are, if you don't get the fuck from in front the door I'ma blast a hole in you!" Mason yelled.

"It's me," Garret yelled, placing Minnie in front of him as a buffer, just in case. "Open the door, man!" He looked back at his soldier. "It's cool. You can put it down now." The man complied and Garret focused back on the door.

"Garret?" Mason said from the other side. "What you doing here?"

"I was coming to tell you what happened with Vanguard."

"Why you in them vans?"

"Because we needed unmarked cars and came straight over here from Vanguard's block!" Garret continued. "Now open the door so I can talk to you." He squeezed Minnie's arm and she screamed. "Plus I got the girl."

A few seconds later, Mason opened the door but twelve barrels were aimed at Garret from inside. Nobody fully trusted him.

"Aye, what ya'll doing," Garret said raising his hands in the air. "We come in peace!" He cut the light off his phone and tucked it in his pocket.

Slowly Mason lowered his gun and yanked Minnie inside, while his sons kept their weapons trained on Garret.

Arlyndo rushed up to Minnie and pulled her into his arms. But she wasn't feeling him and instead wiggled away and sat on the sofa next to Jersey.

Garret walked inside the basement and instructed his man to remain outside.

"What's going on?" Garret asked. "And why the power out?"

"We thought it was an ambush," Mason said.

"Well how you know it ain't?" Garret said playfully.

By T. Styles

Mason frowned. It was a bad joke. "Why you here? We already know Tops ain't hit, Vanguard." He paused. "So what you want?"

BOOM!

Suddenly one of the arcade systems exploded followed by another one inside the basement. It was a light bomb but did some damage as small shards of shrapnel flew everywhere. "RUN!" Mason yelled as everyone hit it for the stairs leading out the basement. "WE UNDER ATTACK!"

"YA'LL CAN GET IN MY VANS!" Garret instructed.

Everyone charged up the dark stairs and toward the foyer.

Once outside, they could hear explosion after explosion as they loaded into the rides.

"What's happening?" Jersey screamed. "I don't understand!"

"Ma, come with me," Howard said placing her in one of the three vans in the driveway where he, Jersey and Patterson piled inside.

Linden, Tops and Arlyndo were easing into another vehicle when suddenly Arlyndo looked around. "Where is Minnie?"

Mason's eyes widened as he looked around. Once again she had gotten away. "Tops, you go after her!"

"I'm on it!" He ran off toward the woods surrounding the property.

BOOM!"

Another explosion let off in the house. "Get in the van, Arlyndo!" Mason yelled shoving him inside. "Now, before the entire house blows."

"What about Minnie?" He continued to scream.

They were the only two standing in the driveway as the remaining vans took off.

Arlyndo's heart was beating as he tried desperately from where he was standing to spot his girl and Tops.

"I need my—"

Mason shoved Arlyndo inside by the back of his head for his own safety.

Once Mason and Arlyndo were inside, the driver took off right before another explosion took out all of the windows. As the vehicles rushed from the property, Mason could think of only one person responsible and he felt stupid for giving him access to his home.

It was too late.

CHAPTER TWENTY-SEVEN
10:03 PM

After setting off the bombs on Mason's estate, destroying his entire home, Banks ran toward the front door with Stretch at his side. He had to hit the road. Normally Rev would be driving but he felt only he could get to Mason's house quickly enough to find Minnie.

Time was of the essence.

The fucked up part was that during all of the excitement, with both men trying to locate Minnie while she was on foot, Ericka had slid in the backseat of the truck.

Banks would've shoved her out himself, but by the time he noticed her he was halfway down the road. There was no time. Instead he sped down the street headed toward Mason's house on a mission.

Stretch kept time with his wife by crawling in the backseat when they spotted her.

After detonating the bombs, so that Minnie could escape, he needed to pick her up.

"I want to ask you both something," Ericka said huffing and puffing from the backseat. She

By T. Styles

had been waiting for them to say something, even if it was why she was there.

But they maintained their silence so she broke first.

Banks glared at her from the rearview mirror.

"Not now, Ericka," Stretch said, keeping his eyes peeled out for Minnie. "You shouldn't even be here."

"Well I have something I want to talk to you both about," she continued.

Banks looked at her periodically from the rearview, but his focus was clear, to find his daughter.

"What is it?" Stretch asked.

"Did you fuck Bet?"

Banks shook his head.

He knew it would eventually come out and he even told Stretch to bring Ericka on board about their agreement. But Stretch feared she would never sign off on him fathering Banks' children, and he really wanted to do the favor for the boss.

Yes he fucked Bet. But Banks was there each time, kissing her lips. For some reason seeing Bet get banged out was easy for Banks. But he knew it would've never gone down with Nikki.

His heart could not take it.

Stretch ran his hand down his face as his chest pounded. "What...what are...you talking about now?" He stuttered.

"You did didn't you?" She asked glaring at him.

Stretch looked out the window. "I can't believe you doing this. When you know what we going through right now. When you know what's at stake."

"Banks, did you know about this?" Ericka continued. "Did you know your wife fucking my husband?"

Silence.

She had her answer.

"You did didn't you?" She felt like the breath had been knocked from her body. Everybody was in on the joke but her. "What's wrong with your dick that you can't get your own wife pregnant?"

Silence.

"I can't believe this," She looked down and cried softly. "I wanted more kids and you gave the Wales many!"

The thing was neither Stretch nor Banks had time for her tears.

"Ericka, I'm warning you," Stretch said.

By T. Styles

His temples throbbed just thinking about how this would fuck up things for him and Banks' already torn relationship. He had worked so hard to seal his position and now all he did was cause Banks grief.

"You warning me and so what?" She yelled like a maniac. Her eyes were red and tears streamed down her face, leaving tracks in her makeup. "Fuck you think you gonna do to me?"

Banks considered pulling over and yanking her out, but again she wasn't priority. But Stretch had better do something soon, or he would.

"Ericka, please, don't make me hurt you," Stretch said. "Please."

Ericka laughed harder, her voice sounded like a thousand nails running down a chalkboard. "You don't have the fucking balls to do anything to me. You about a stupid ass—"

Suddenly Stretch wrapped his hands around her neck, crawled on top of her and squeezed.

"Fuck is you doing?" Banks yelled, for the first time breaking his silence.

But this time Stretch wasn't answering the boss.

He snapped.

And there was no turning back as he unleashed everything he felt that moment. Disappointment in himself for betraying Banks, an extreme irritation with his wife and the pressure of failure.

"Fuck...you," Stretch continued as he squeezed harder. "Fuck you!"

Although Banks was annoyed, for some reason her silent death put him at ease. He needed peace and received it with each squeeze. And as a result he was able to make it to the perimeter of Mason's house, without further interruption.

When he was as close as he could be to the Lou's demolished property without detection, he parked on the side of a dark road and turned out the lights.

For a moment he and Stretch stared at one another.

"She's dead," Stretch said, as sweat rolled down his forehead. That was evident. "I killed her. I fucking killed her."

"We'll dump her later." Banks said. "For now let's go find my kid."

By T. Styles

CHAPTER TWENTY-EIGHT

Deep in the woods, Tops could see his prey. He had been tailing her from afar all night.

Her presence would've gone unnoticed to a less keen eye. Mainly because she crept. Still, her heavy breathing, laced with knowing that death was imminent, stuck out like blood in white snow.

But something else was happening.

As he watched her move frantically, through the rough thickets, he grew aroused. Some would say if the past dictated the future, his actions weren't his fault. Besides, he became a mad man at the age of twelve, when he saw his grandmother strangle his mother, her daughter, with bare hands. Just to gain access to a monthly welfare check. Instead of being horrified, he relished in seeing his mother take her last breath and longed for that sensation ever since.

It wasn't like she was the best person in the world to begin with.

Tops' mother, a Jewish woman with thick blonde hair, had given her soul to crack cocaine, forsaking all others. Because of the lack of parenting skills, he had been passed around to women looking to get sexual gratification from a boy child.

But seeing his mother's murder vindicated his dark soul.

As he watched Minnie try to escape with her life, he dipped into his pants and past his bushy hair. When he found what he was looking for, he grabbed his sweaty damp penis, and nudged it as a woman would her alcoholic husband who was late for work.

Within seconds he was aroused as he watched a frightened Wales from afar.

Within the woods, Minnie had gone as far as she could.

Sweat poured down her face, blurring her view as she focused on the steep hill that would consume her if she fell into it. She was about to go back where she came, toward Mason's mansion, figuring they were gone. But when she

By T. Styles

saw Tops jerking off behind her, fear struck her to the core.

Afraid for more than just her life, in one horrifying moment she understood everything her father tried to shield her from. From showing her how to fight, to warning her to be careful who she gave her heart to...Banks made sure she was prepared for this moment. And now she regretted the day she ever separated from those who loved her.

If she were to survive, she swore she would rise and be a queen whether in coke or any other venture she tackled in life.

Just to make Banks proud.

And if she ever saw him again, she would wrap her arms around him and tell him she was sorry.

"Who are you?" She screamed at Tops. "What are you doing?"

An owl hooted.

He remained silent, as he jerked his long hairy penis.

"What you want from me?" She yelled louder.

"A taste." Tops said in a voice so deep, it rocked the sleeping fowl above in the trees.

With eyes planted on him as he inched closer, branches crackling under his feet, she backed up without considering what she knew. That behind her was a steep black hole that was waiting to devour her.

And still, struck with fear, she moved her left foot rearward and plunged into the darkness.

Screaming all the way.

Banks crept through the brush on the outskirts of Mason's property. Knowing full well that if Mason or one of his goons spotted him it would be the equivalent of being the sole winner in a billion dollar lottery.

They wanted him that badly.

But what could he do?

At the end of the day he would put his life on the line to find his daughter and that's exactly what he was doing.

"You sure she out here?" Stretch whispered, walking behind Banks a little too closely.

"Because, because, it looks like she wouldn't be here, man. I think we should go back."

Silence.

"Because it's mostly, mostly dark out...out now," Stretch stuttered. "Don't seem smart for her to be out alone. Yeah, I think we should definitely leave and come back when it's light out."

Banks continued to push through the dark woods surrounding the Lou's property. Of course he heard Stretch, but he was done with him a long time ago. From the moment he let loose that his kids were born from his sperm, he secretly started hating him. Not because he was jealous. Banks was far from envious.

He despised Stretch because he had handled his secret recklessly, and that brought his family undue stress.

"What's that over there?" Stretch asked, eyes wide with fright. "I think I saw something moving, man. You don't think its Mason and them do you?" Although he was talking non-stop, what he was really trying to do was keep his mind off the fact that he murdered his wife.

And what was he going to tell his daughter?

Shay already showed characteristics of being a troublemaker in the making. Without her mother, what would become of her now? He couldn't be the father she needed while also worrying about falling out of Banks' good graces.

"I think we should go back, Banks. You know I always tell you the truth. I think we should—"

"Shhh!" Banks yelled, throwing a palm in his face when he heard a noise.

Stretch's eyes widened more as he tried to see through the trees and darkness. "What is it?" He whispered. "What you hear? You think you see, Minnie?"

Banks glared at him. The constant chattering was more than annoying. It was crippling.

"Sorry, man," Stretch continued. "I'm just worried that's all."

Banks moved further into the woods, toward the sound. He could hear branches breaking and wondered if his daughter was near. When the sound grew louder, he moved quicker but halted when he saw a family of deer nearby.

Seeing Banks and Stretch, they hopped away.

"Fuck," Banks said under his breath. All hope was gone.

By T. Styles

"What you wanna do now?" Stretch asked, wishing he would say go home.

"Let's go back," Banks said.

Relieved, Stretch smiled and turned around. But the moment his back was turned, Banks reached into his waist and removed a .45 handgun. Pointing it at Stretch's head, he pulled the trigger.

Without hesitation.

Annihilating the birth father of his children.

Blood splattered against his face, similar to when Dennis killed Arlyn. Much was evident in that moment. In a twist, Banks was becoming his father. The man he had grown to hate.

Now...

Where was Minnie?

CHAPTER TWENTY-NINE

Mason paced the floor of one of his many decrepit houses in Baltimore city. Inside the room was Garret and Linden who were waiting on news from Tops.

Did he find Minnie or not?

When Tops finally pulled up, everyone focused on the door as he walked inside. His body was so large his head brushed against the crest of the doorway. And the pressures of his steps were so heavy they made indentions in the floor as he moved.

Standing before them he took a deep breath. "It's done."

Mason frowned. "What you mean *it's done*?"

"What you asked me to do." Tops said. "I'm telling you I took care of her."

Mason wiped his hand down his face. Was he hearing him correctly? "Hold up, you telling me you killed...that you killed Minnie?"

Silence.

"Say something, man." Linden said. "Ain't nobody paying you to stand there and look—"

"Yeah!" Tops nodded. "I killed her okay."

Everyone wiped hands down their faces.

"I told you to bring her to me!" Mason roared. "Why would you kill the one person we could use as collateral? And so soon? Don't you realize that nigga got my son?"

Tops shrugged. "She was trying to get away and—"

"And what?" Mason yelled, stepping up to him. Although his gaze had to move upward since Tops was so tall, it didn't stop the rage from pumping through his veins.

"I think you need to calm down," Tops warned looking down at him. "ASAP."

"Or what, nigga?" Mason continued.

Tops took a deep breath and he was preparing to yoke him.

And then he looked at Linden, whose hand hovered over his weapon, along with Garret who was doing the same. If shit kicked off he would die twice in that room. Taking a deep breath he said, "I didn't have a choice, man. That's all I can say."

"I can't believe this."

"There's a way out," Garret interrupted. "I mean, we talked about it before but now...now we can use it to our advantage."

"I know we not talking about lying to the nigga again," Linden said.

"Why not?" Garret asked throwing his hands up. "We don't have her and he got Derrick. We need some leverage."

"I don't think it's a good idea, man," Linden said to Mason. "I told you this before when it came up. And I'm telling you now."

Mason thought about his options.

He didn't have many.

On one hand Banks had his son, and although he was sure he wouldn't hurt him, he didn't know what lying about having Minnie would do to an already tight situation.

"I think you should lie too," Tops said.

"Where is her body?" Mason questioned, trying to catch his breath.

"What body?"

Mason shifted in place. Fuck body he thought he was talking about? "You said you killed Minnie right?" He paused. "So where is she?"

"Oh, so, so she fell in a ditch."

Mason glared. "So you don't got her corpse?"

"Sorry, man. I didn't wanna be lugging no dead weight around. I figured the vultures would eat her anyway. But we should be good."

"Did this nigga say *WE?*" Mason snapped. "*WE* ain't the one out here beefing. *WE* ain't got a son in this nigga's possession. I do!"

"We gonna work it out," Linden said.

Mason wiped his hand down his face.

"What you wanna do, Mason?" Garret asked. "You gotta tell us something. Because if you ask me, he still think you got her. Might as well play it up."

Harris walked down the hallway of the mansion looking for his father when he happened upon Banks' office. Going through the door he saw his brother sitting behind a computer looking intently at the screen.

Moving further inside, he closed the door. "What you doing in Pop's office?" He plopped on the sofa across from the desk. "I thought you couldn't stand him."

"Ain't you supposed to be in the basement?"

"Man, Pops soldiers don't care no more. They all know we leaving. Basically they riding the clock out." He yawned. "Now what you doing?"

Spacey sighed. "He got me working on something."

Harris nodded. "So you ain't mad no more?"

Spacey shrugged. "I don't care."

Harris laughed. "But you do though."

Spacey leaned back in Banks' chair. It squeaked. "You saying you really, *really* ain't mad that pops a—"

"Woman?"

"Don't make me say it."

"I ain't saying I ain't mad." Harris shrugged. "I mean I am fucked up by it."

"That's it?" Spacey scratched his scalp. "Just fucked up?"

"I ain't really had a chance to think about it beyond that," Harris continued. "Are they lesbians or—"

"Fuck!" Spacey yelled, cutting him off.

Harris frowned. "What's wrong with you now?"

"I'm grossed the fuck out."

Harris laughed. "I get that, I do, but what's a father?"

"Ain't nobody trying to—"

220   *By T. Styles*

"What's a father?" Harris repeated.

"I know what you doing, Harris."

"All I'm saying is that Pops been there." He shrugged. "And as long as I'm not thinking about what they *doing* in the bedroom I'm good."

Spacey focused back on the computer.

"What you watching?"

"Some recordings from earlier, at the Lou's." Spacey responded.

"You know that's a violation of code 18.US.2511? To be eavesdropping on niggas right?"

"What, man?"

"It's a federal law to participate in interception and disclosure of wire, oral and electronics. We can get jail time for this shit."

"In a minimum security prison," Spacey said.

"Prison time is still prison time," Harris corrected him. "Ain't nobody trying to—"

"Wow..." Spacey said to himself, while scratching his scalp.

"What now?"

"I just realized something. Pops been planning this shit forever."

"What you mean?"

"The escape." Spacey paused. "Think about it...I got a degree in computer science, which means I know how to get into niggas systems, video cameras and you know—"

"Law." Harris said completing his sentence. "He got me in a magnet high school where I study law."

"Meanwhile Joey knows the drug business." Spacey continued. "Minnie the only one not worth shit, and she the one causing him the most struggle."

"She gonna come around," Harris said smiling. "But pops crazy."

"Crazy?" Spacey snapped. "He using us!"

"That nigga brilliant!"

"For now," Spacey said. "Cause if you ask me, we ain't seen the worst of what he's capable of doing. But get ready."

By T. Styles

CHAPTER THIRTY
11:01 PM

The road back seemed heavy.

Banks had failed to bring his daughter home and more than it all, he didn't know where she was. He was starting to feel like a failure in all he tried to do.

A failure as a husband.

A failure as a father.

A failure as a business owner.

Defeated, he pulled up in his driveway, past the many soldiers covering his property and parked. Immediately his phone rang. When he recognized the number he sighed. It was Mason and he didn't feel like talking. Banks was pretty sure he didn't have Minnie yet.

Besides, he saw her run on the cameras.

But what if he was wrong?

So he answered.

"What?" Banks ran his hand down his beard.

"Aye, you remember Mrs. Porter?" Mason asked. "From high school?"

Banks sunk into the soft leather driver's seat. "Yeah. The broad with the red curly wig right?"

Mason laughed hard. "Nigga...she was rocking that shit like it was official."

"That's cause we siced her up," Banks responded. "Telling her how phat she was and shit." He shook his head. "You know I saw her on the corner a few years ago and she still wearing it right? We probably should've told her back then."

"Yo, fuck that bitch," Mason continued. "She ain't like me until..."

"Until what?" Banks wiped his hand down his face.

"Until I let her suck my dick." He paused. "You know she was my second right?"

"You always did lie."

"Never." Mason said seriously. "I never lie."

"Just shield the truth," Banks said.

Silence.

"What you want, Mason?" Banks asked getting back to the heart of the matter. "In case you forgot, we at war."

"I got Minnie."

Banks heart rocked inside his chest upon hearing the words. All of his hopes for his daughter being free deflated in that moment. "You really don't wanna lie to me."

"I'm not lying."

By T. Styles

"Like you lied before?" Banks paused. "When you told me you had her? When my people already snatched her off the street?"

"I have her this time, man," Mason continued.

Banks felt it was best to call his bluff. "You lying because my daughter in my house."

"Trust me, man, she not," Mason said. "And if you don't give me Derrick, personally, I will—"

"Aye, Mason, don't threaten me."

"And what if—"

Banks angrily pushed open the car door and moved quickly inside his house. He was walking so fast that had somebody got in his path they would've been knocked over. Luckily Bet moved to his right or she would've been first.

"What's wrong?" Bet asked as he shoved her to the side. "You got Minnie?"

He wasn't about to answer dumb questions. If he had her where would she be hiding? In his ass?

Ignoring her, Banks grabbed large scissors from the kitchen and then moved to where Derrick lay in the bedroom. He knocked the food off the trey he was eating and placed the phone in a position so Mason could hear everything.

Then he hit the speakerphone.

Curious, Bet and four of Banks' men entered the room also, each trying to figure out what was happening.

"Unc, what's wrong?" Derrick asked Banks seeing his angry energy.

Banks grabbed his foot as two of Banks men held Derrick down. Although he was still nursing a bullet wound, they didn't want to take a chance of Derrick being strong enough to fight back.

"You on the phone, nigga!" Banks yelled at Mason. "I want you to hear this shit! 'Cause this for you!"

"Aye, Banks, don't hurt my son!"

"OR WHAT?" Banks screamed. "OR...WHAT?" With that he cut off Derrick's big toe and watched it plop to the floor.

Derrick's screaming caused Mason to yell to the Gods for revenge but nothing helped.

The damage was done.

On full rage mode, Banks jerked his gun from his waist and pressed it firmly against Derrick's head. He cocked it and said, "I got my heat on this nigga! Now do you—"

"Banks, don't kill—"

"Do you got my daughter?" Banks said, cutting Mason off.

By T. Styles

"Please don't shoot me," Derrick begged, his hands in the air. "Please!"

"DO YOU HAVE MINNIE?" Banks yelled, huffing and puffing. "DO YOU GOT MY DAUGHTER?"

"I don't have her!" Mason shouted. "Please, Banks...don't do it." He paused. "Don't kill my son."

Silence.

Sweat poured down Banks' face as he repositioned his gun in his waist. Take a deep breath he said, "Don't ever threaten me again."

With blood on his hand, literally, Banks grabbed his phone and ended the call.

Bet passed out.

The moment the call was over, Mason tossed the cell phone down on the sofa. Slowly he rose and walked toward Garret. Without hesitation, he shot him in the center of the forehead, due to the bad advice. Next he moved his gun to Linden whose eyes widened and hands rose in the air.

"Please don't, man," Linden said, fearing he was next. "I'm...I'm your brother."

Breathing heavily, and with the look of rage in his eyes, Mason lowered the gun slowly before flopping on the sofa. It was too late in the night to be killing brothers.

Linden took several deep breaths while Tops shook his head, running a hand down his face. It was a close call.

But neither could say they didn't understand why Mason was angry. But still, looking at a body on the floor was stressful, seeing as though they never predicted his erratic move.

"That nigga was dumb anyway," Mason said referring to Garret. The truth was he felt stupid for having let Garret convince him to lie. Also, he wanted to know how Banks was so sure he didn't have her.

He was missing something.

The cameras.

But he didn't know.

"I have a plan," Linden said.

"I don't wanna hear no more plans," Mason said.

"This one you'll wanna hear," he said. "I know somebody who can give us an advantage. A huge advantage."

Mason sat back and looked over at him. "Who?"

"I figure we been going about shit the wrong way," Linden paused. "Banks smarter than we giving him credit for."

"Nigga, get to the part I should give a fuck about."

Linden sighed. "The only thing Banks cares about is getting on a plane. So to cripple him, we need to destroy the dream."

"That's what the fuck I been trying to do."

"I know, but we have to go a different way," Linden said. "Listen, I know this Jamaican cat named Whoyawanmetabe."

Mason frowned. "What the fuck?"

"He's expensive," Linden continued. "But he's good."

Whoyawanmetabe was a unique individual. He never gave a price until much later, after the job was over and done. People loved using him when under pressure, but most of his clients regretted ever meeting him afterwards, and Mason would soon find out why.

Breathing heavily Mason said, "Call him."

"Are you sure?"

"Call him." Mason's nostrils flared.

Within twenty minutes, Whoyawanmetabe entered and stepped over Garret's body as if all was well. His dreads were neat and long and ran down his back. Every time he moved it smelled of coconut. But his presence was that of a powerful island king.

Mason walked up to him, curious as to how he could help. Besides, Linden gave so little information on the mysterious being. "What kind of name is Whoyawanmetabe?"

Whoyawanmetabe laughed. "That's not me birth name." His accent was as rich as a batch of ganja from Jamaica.

Mason frowned and looked at his brother and then Tops. "Then why they call you that?"

"Because I'm a masta of gettin' the job done, ya no?" He said in a heavy accent. "So when me walk into a room, the first ting me ask is, who yah want me to be?"

Mason smiled. "Okay."

"So now me ask...who ya want me to be to you?"

11:33 PM

When Mason walked through the door of one of his other homes, Jersey was cooking fried chicken, mashed potatoes and green beans. His sons Patterson and Howard were sitting on the sofa watching TV. But since news was on, which they hated, he figured the set was watching them instead.

Arlyndo sat in a recliner in the corner of the room with his hoodie pulled up over his head. He was sulking about how he lured Minnie to be taken. And more than it all that his father refused to tell him where she was.

"Any word on Derrick?" Howard asked.

Of course there was word. He had been injured, because of his stupidity. So since none of the information was good he elected to remain silent to his family.

Mason shook his head no.

"You think he gonna be okay?" Patterson asked.

"My son's a fighter," Jersey said, her face still bloated and bruised. "Like me." She looked at Mason before focusing back on cooking. "So trust me, he's gonna be fine."

Mason could still barely look at her face. The guilt weighed on him harder in his sober hours.

But she seemed to not care.

After making all of their plates, including Mason's, Jersey sat and watched them eat. She didn't have a thing.

Besides, it was a special meal. One of a kind. And so, within twenty minutes, every one of them were knocked out, courtesy of mama.

Hearing them snore, she grabbed her cell phone and made a call.

"They sleep."

"I'm on my way."

Ten minutes later Dragon White, her foster brother, entered the house with three of his friends. He was 6'3 and his white skin was bronzed. Extremely attractive, his looks were like poison and had pulled many women into their detriment. "Which ones are my nephews?" He asked her.

By T. Styles

"Over there," she said pointing her sons out.

"And that's the one who hurt you?" Dragon paused, glaring at Mason with extreme hate. "Your...the nigga you married?" His nostrils flared.

Silence.

Dragon took a deep breath and looked at his friends. "Take my nephews to the van."

One by one they lifted the young men up and carried them to the waiting vehicle. When they were done, the men waited outside for their next orders.

"Why would you leave me like that, Jersey?" Dragon said passionately. "And why you don't see fit to call, 'cept you need help?"

"It's been over twenty years. You still talking about that?" She paused. "Besides, you know why. You hurt me."

"Have I ever hurt you like this?" He placed his cool hand on her bruised and battered face. "I mean look at you. It looks like you been boxing. We may have had our problems but I never hit you, Jersey. I would—"

"Stop," she said softly, a single tear tracing alongside her face.

"Don't tell me to stop," he glared. "I'm your brother."

"You really wanna go there? You really wanna pretend like you ain't make me suck your—"

"I thought you wanted to. You should have wanted to make me feel good." He took a deep breath and looked around from where he stood. The past they could get into later. It was time for business. "Go get in the van."

"What you 'bout to do?"

"Nothing." Dragon said, looking at Mason with envy.

"Don't hurt him." She paused. "I love him. And he's still my husband."

Why she say that? It only made matters worse.

Dragon gritted his teeth.

She touched his arm. "Please."

He nodded and took a deep breath. "Go wait outside."

Reluctantly she walked out.

Now alone, slowly he moved toward Mason who was sleeping on the sofa with his mouth wide open. Dragon knew the drugs he gave his foster sister would put the man out for at least a couple of hours. But even he was surprised at how hard Mason was sleeping.

In Mason's condition, Dragon could do anything he desired.

Sure he heard his foster sister when she said don't touch him, but he could care less about her wants and needs. What about the pain he was in? Here lied the man who had taken Jersey from him, causing him extreme distress over the years. When she first went missing, Dragon went mad, believing her boyfriend killed her.

Originally he thought it was his fault too. Because the argument Jersey and her boyfriend got into, the night Mason met her, was due to Dragon calling her man on the phone and threatening to kill him if he ever laid a hand on her again.

It wasn't until she reached out earlier that night, that he knew she was alive. And had elected to ignore him all those years.

Removing a switchblade from his hip, he lowered his height to slice Mason's throat open. The blade dug into his skin just as one of his men walked back inside.

"We ready to—" The man stopped mid sentence, witnessing what was about to take place.

Murder.

Dragon stood up, wiped the blood from the blade on his jeans and glared at him. "I thought I told you to wait in the car."

He nodded and rushed out.

Dragon hit the button on the switchblade, lowering its height before tucking it back into his pocket. "You one lucky ass nigga." He paused. "For now."

Before leaving, he removed his dick and pissed all over Mason's face and inside his mouth as he slept peacefully. As the urine dampened his hair and body, he smiled. When he was totally relieved, he walked out, closing the door behind him.

Two hours later, Mason awoke groggy and with an extreme headache. He was also taken aback by the smell that lingered around him and the horrible taste in his mouth. Holding his head and neck, he stumbled to the bathroom to look at himself in the mirror. He figured he must've been in a fight because the last thing he remembered was eating and then he was out cold.

By T. Styles

Standing in front of the mirror, and witnessing the gash on his neck, he figured he knew what happened.

He reasoned that Jersey, still angry at how he beat her, pissed on him before cutting his throat.

He was wrong.

After taking a shower, brushing his teeth, getting dressed and patching his neck, he thought about his wife again. Something about the new woman she was presenting had him feeling some kind of way.

Was she as vicious as he was and he didn't know until now? After all these years?

When his cell phone rang, he answered.

It was Jersey.

"What up?" He scratched his chin.

"You hurt me," Jersey said softly.

Just hearing her voice made his dick jump. "I know."

"I could've had you killed, Mason." She paused. "You don't...you don't know how..." She couldn't complete her sentence. "You don't know me. The *real* me."

"Do you still love me?" He asked.

Silence.

"Is it worth it?" She asked. "The drugs and the money? Is it worth losing your family?"

He took a deep breath. "I'm not losing my family." He said confidently. "But you got my sons right?"

"Yes. They're mad at me though."

"Why?"

"I drugged them too. Figured it was the only way they would come with me."

"Jersey," he said wiping his hand down his face. "You should've asked them. Fuck you drug 'em for?"

She cried harder.

"Listen," he continued. "We gonna be okay. And I know you don't believe me but...I mean...just...just don't give up on family yet. Let me get out of this. And then let's make a decision on us together."

"Find my son first, Mason," she paused. "You can't even talk to me without him."

She hung up.

By T. Styles

CHAPTER THIRTY-ONE

Vanguard's head was throbbing as he paced the living room while talking to his wife on the phone.

Claire Morton was a wreck just thinking about having to leave the country and move with a *pack of niggers* on an island she'd never seen. And she wasted no time telling him either. "I don't trust them blackies!" Claire yelled. "I don't want to leave my friends! And family!"

"Claire, please," Vanguard begged. "Don't you understand? If we don't leave then—"

"Banks and his wife are drug dealers!" She continued dominating the conversation as usual. "And I don't do drug dealers! Evil is in black people's DNA, that's why their skin is dark as their souls."

"But..."

Suddenly the lights went out in their home.

"Vanguard!" She yelled on the phone. "Do you hear me?"

"Claire, the power has gone out," he said walking through the house. It was completely dark. "I have to call the electric company."

"I don't trust it," she said. "Something feels off."

"Give me a few minutes," he said. "But please reconsider. Banks tells me the island is beautiful and we could start our lives over. In paradise."

He ended the call and opened his front door where two armed men stood on guard, as Banks promised, after his brother was murdered.

"Everything alright, sir?" One of the men asked politely.

"The power is out," Vanguard frowned, scratching his head. "You seen anything out here?"

"No. You want me to call BG&E?"

"No...uh...I'll do it." He smiled and closed the door.

After making the call, twenty minutes later a black man with dreads that ran down his back appeared at the door. When Vanguard looked out on the street, he saw a marked van from the utility company. But he was still very suspicious after his twin died.

"Sir, did you call about your power?" Whoyawanmetabe asked.

Vanguard smiled when he recognized a London accent from his hometown. How was he

By T. Styles

to know that Whoyawanmetabe was a master at over twenty languages and accents, which was another reason he was paid the price he demanded?

"You're from London?"

Whoyawanmetabe smiled. "All my life." He paused. "May I?" He pointed into the house.

"Oh, of course." Vanguard laughed. It felt so good to hear a taste of his hometown that he almost forgot the purpose of the visit. "Please, please come inside."

Whoyawanmetabe complied and looked around from where he stood. "Can you tell me where the circuit breaker is?"

"Sure...it's downstairs."

"Cheers. I'll walk around to check a few things and then head to your breaker afterwards."

"Whatever you need."

Whoyawanmetabe nodded and walked away and Vanguard flopped on the sofa, before calling his wife twenty minutes later. Slightly relieved that his small troubles would be over soon, and the power would be restored, he turned his attention to his wife.

"Claire."

"Did the power come back on?"

"No...but listen," he paused. "I can't make you go with me." He took a deep breath. "And as much as I want you to, I understand if you would prefer to stay."

"Then I'm staying."

The moment she said those words, his stomach rocked and he felt the urge to shit. She had called him on his bluff. "Claire, please don't do this."

"You heard what I said." She paused. "You leave with that nigger to a place you don't know and I'm gone. Forever."

Suddenly the lights came back on but it didn't matter.

His world was destroyed.

"Claire, I have to go," he took a deep breath, holding his stomach. "I'll call you back."

When Whoyawanmetabe came out, he walked up to Vanguard. "Everything is okay now."

"That was quick," Vanguard smiled. "Do you know what happened?"

"Sometimes power surges in surrounding areas and it may offset the grid. But don't worry. Everything is going to be fine." He shook his hand. "Have a nice night."

By T. Styles

After Vanguard walked him out, he quickly moved to the bathroom. His stomach churned as he thought about losing his brother and now possibly his wife. Suddenly going out of the country with Banks seemed stupid. He didn't even know the man.

Even if the airport forced him into early retirement, it wasn't like he didn't have a cushy fund to put him and his wife up for the rest of their lives.

So he considered staying put.

But what was he going to tell Banks?

Taking a deep breath, he released the biggest dump he had in his life. The relief was so immediate that suddenly he had high hopes for the future.

Standing up, he looked at the brown monster floating inside. "Pew," he said waving his hand, as if someone else did it. Extending his fingertips, he tapped the flusher and then...

BOOM!

Banks stood in front of Bet, Joey, Spacey and Harris in the living room. With his hands in his pockets he took a deep breath. "If things go my way, I'm taking you all to the island tonight," he said. "It's settled with Vanguard already."

Their eyes widened. "What about my daughter?" Bet asked, her head slightly tender from passing out on the floor earlier.

"I'm coming back to get her. I just wanna make sure everyone else is there first."

"Pops, I don't want you out here alone," Joey said.

"Me either," Harris added. "It don't seem smart."

"I get that but I can't risk something happening to you all too. So I'm gonna make a few moves out on the street and then we leaving."

"And what about Ericka?" Bet asked. "And Stretch?"

"And Shay?" Harris asked, clearing his throat.

"I don't know where Stretch or his wife is," Banks lied. "And Shay is coming with us."

Spacey, Harris and Joey looked at each other in confusion about Stretch and Ericka's disappearance.

By T. Styles

Bet, on the other hand, knew her husband was lying. She had been with him enough to know that Stretch was gone for life. And after the way his wife performed in her office, her only thought was, *Good riddance.*

"This move seems reckless," Bet said. "I mean, how do you know Vanguard will want to leave this early?"

"He doesn't have a choice."

"What does that mean, Banks?"

RING. RING. RING.

Banks removed his cell phone from his pocket and took a deep breath. It was a number he didn't recognize. But since Minnie was out there somewhere, again he had to answer all calls.

"Hello."

"You nigger!"

He frowned. "Who the fuck is this?" He yelled, when he heard a white woman's voice.

"Dad, what's wrong?" Harris asked as all three of Banks' sons stood up and walked toward him.

Banks put up a finger for them to quiet. "Who on this phone?" Suddenly he could hear the woman crying and in that moment, all made sense. "Claire, what's happening?"

"They fucking killed my husband!" He yelled. "Do you hear me? They put a bomb in my house and killed my husband! And it's all your fault!"

As Claire laid out everything she knew, beginning with the power outage, Banks was stunned. To make matters worse, Mason had successfully fucked up his plans to fly out again. And it also looked like they used a common friend with a lot of power...Whoyawanmetabe.

The thing was, when Linden was mad at Mason years ago, it was he who put Banks on to the Jamaican. Through Stretch dropping off the money to Linden when he had fallen out of Mason's graces. Now it registered that he gave his brother the connection too.

As Banks reflected, he realized he was going about things the wrong way with Mason. He had to be smarter and to not allow his Minnie going missing to come in the way of getting the others to safety.

So as he allowed her to yell, alternating between racist rants and cries, he grew clearer on his plans.

Banks' only goal was to get to his island.

But he knew his friend's goals too.

By T. Styles

When the smoke was clear, he knew the first thing Mason would do was work on rebuilding his organization and find a new connect.

But what if there was no brand left?

Banks had to cripple it beyond repair.

So he made the call.

CHAPTER THIRTY-TWO
SUNDAY
2:37 AM

Leonard was sitting in a dog park watching his two grey Pitbulls have a night of it. While most single men used their free time palavering with women, when Leonard wasn't working for Mason pumping cocaine on the streets, he dedicated most of his time to the animals he raised since birth.

But Leonard was hardworking too.

Which is why Mason entrusted him with key points of his business. Not only because he knew cocaine better than most Columbians, but also because he was both respected and feared by the men he ruled. And so with him on his team, Mason's business flourished.

When his phone rang he answered it, taking his eyes off his animals in the process. "Hello." He gripped his dick before yawning.

A seductress asked, "What you doing?"

When he heard the woman's sweet voice, his body rocked. Besides, it had been a few days since he had something soft and her tone was like

By T. Styles

an alarm to the rest of his body, mainly his dick. "I don't know...who is this?"

"You know who it is," she said. "I mean, we fucked a few times but I couldn't be that bad where you would forget me."

Leonard thought about all the women he smashed in the past few months. Since most were uneventful, he shrugged. She could have been anybody. But it didn't mean he wasn't willing to give her another try, whoever she was. "You gotta tell me more than that."

"Okay...I made you cum in two minutes."

He wiped his hand down his face. This was getting interesting. "Is that right?" He groped himself. "And where you do that at?"

"Your car."

Now the possible women were narrowed down to about twenty, but still he was coming up short. "Okay, okay...so how about we do this, you meet me at..."

He stopped talking in midsentence.

Where were his dogs?

"Hello." She said. "You there?"

Leonard leaped up, his head rotating from left to right.

"I gotta go." He said to the caller before hanging up, as he looked from where he stood for his animals.

The woman could care either which way if he left. Her job was done.

"Jekyll and Hyde!" He yelled.

Still he saw nothing.

"Jekyll and Hyde! Come here!"

On the hunt for his dogs, he ran toward the woods outlining the park.

He found them.

Thirty feet behind the trees, his heart tripped a few beats when he saw his animals lying on their sides, with their tongues out of their mouths. Clumps of tainted ground beef around them. Devastated, he dropped down and pulled his dead animals toward him, one resting on each thigh.

Bad move.

In his grief, he couldn't recognize the trap.

And so with his guard down, a Wales soldier crept up behind him, and put him out of his misery.

For life.

By T. Styles

Brewer was on his second run to Green Burger for one of his regular visits. He kept a tight schedule and for him every minute counted. A lieutenant in Mason's organization, he commanded over fifty-six soldiers himself. He was smart, but not when hungry. Still, his keen ability to know when someone was lying was what drew Mason to him.

Before Brewer stepped into Mason's camp, the men were not as efficient under another lieutenant's employ. But Brewer got them in line quick, and as a result his small block real estate quadrupled in size.

To say he was valuable to Mason would be an understatement.

"Hey, hey Mr. Brewer," the cashier said, her mood much different than in the past. "The...the same...same right?" She stuttered.

"You okay?"

She nodded, although she looked terrified. "Yes, yes, sir. I'm fine."

"You sure?" He paused. "Ain't nobody fucking with you are they?" He joked.

"I'm...I'm fine." She said as tears traced down her face.

He took a deep breath. He liked the little girl, true enough, but outside of giving him his food, they didn't have a bond. So he felt it best to let the matter go.

While she went to search for the food, Brewer received a call on his phone. He was about to see who was hitting him when he heard another voice in the drive thru window.

"Your order's ready," a male said.

Brewer frowned. "Where Tricia?"

"She right here," with that the cashier raised a white paper bag filled with food, which concealed a .45 and shot through it. He didn't stand a chance. The bullet entered Brewer's skull, killing him instantly.

Just that quickly, another one hit the dust.

Amos was digging the walls out of her pussy.

His cell phone was ringing off the hook, but he was feeling too good to answer. Whoever was hitting him would have to wait.

Lying on top of her warm brown body, his hands snaked behind her as he grabbed her ass cheeks, pulling outward. This did nothing but open her pussy wider, allowing him to go deeper, the way he liked.

Although time was of the essence, as a general in Mason's camp, he figured he could tap some fresh ass right quick and then get back to the trap without missing a thump. He was not as important to Mason's camp as Brewer and Leonard, but with losing them both, his murder would cripple Mason beyond repair.

"Damn, why you gotta be wet all the time though?" He asked as he bit his bottom lip. "Fuck." He wasn't even looking at her face. He was all about the pussy. Had he focused on her one time, just once, he would've noticed that her mood was off.

"You like this, baby?" She asked, her voice as dry as a brick wall.

"Love it!" He continued to pump harder. "But I'm almost there." He said. "You gotta push into me a little harder though." He continued. "I ain't feeling it yet."

"Okay," she said. "I'll—"

POP! POP! POP!

Thinking he was hearing things, he was about to ask what was the noise. But his question seemed dumb when he noticed a hole through her forehead, which allowed blood to pour out like a stream from a fountain. Realizing he was under seize, he rolled off her body, just before another bullet entered her torso.

It was evident.

Somebody under the bed was trying to assassinate him.

On his feet, he snatched his weapon off the table and started firing toward the mattress. He didn't know if he hit anybody or not, because by the time he decided to look back, he was sitting in his car butt naked, speeding away from her house.

Now miles down the highway, he used his car cell phone to dial a number. Within a few seconds Mason answered. "Aye, boss, we under attack!"

"I know," he paused. "I been hitting you for hours! Get the men off the streets!"

But it was too late.

By T. Styles

Banks had killed every important soldier but Amos.

His operation had been demolished in a matter of hours.

CHAPTER THIRTY-THREE

Banks sat in his office drinking a bottle of vodka. His recent actions of attacking Mason's soldiers proved successful but were also a distraction. Yes he handicapped his once good friend's operation, but in the end it didn't bring him any closer to finding out where Minnie was, or in getting his family to Wales Island.

At the end of the day Mason's move of killing Vanguard hurt. He needed that plane.

Taking a deep breath, from a secure line, he called the one person he didn't want to.

"Banks Wales," Nidia said hearing his voice on the phone.

"Nidia," he slurred a little.

"I didn't think you'd be returning back to me this early." She paused. "Although I must admit, I'm pleased you did."

Banks sighed. "I'm not coming back."

"Then why are you calling?" She said in a dark tone.

"Nidia, I know...I mean...I know you don't want me to leave." He paused. "And I'm fucked up by that, because we did a lot of good business together."

"What I want is for your happiness. Even if that's not your desire for me."

"I need you to let me access one of your planes. For a month or so. I have to make some trips back and forth."

She laughed.

He sat back in his chair and frowned. "Fuck so funny?"

"You have everything a king could desire and yet you purchased one plane?"

The power of her words hurt and rang true at the same time. Banks never thought about buying more than one plane because he wasn't a flashy type dude. He purchased the plane he loved. And one that would provide extreme comfort for the flight his family had ahead of them. But prior to this moment, he never saw the need to by two until now. Even with his cars, although nice, he only bought what he required.

"I messed up."

"Yes." She paused. "You did. But I'll help you."

His eyes widened and he sat the bottle on his desk. "I thought you'd say no."

"Maybe you should think of me differently. Perhaps you don't realize how much I adore you."

Feeling relieved, he wiped his hand down his face. "Can you have one of your pilots fly it out to the airport I use? And then—"

"Slow down, Captain Wales. We haven't spoken of what I need yet."

He leaned back into his chair. "What is it?"

"You. I want you. And this time I don't want part of you, Banks Wales. I want you sexually and mentally too. You come with me, and I will have your family taken wherever you desire. And together we will build an even bigger empire."

Her words did make him think. If he threw himself on his sword, and gave her what she wanted, then his family would be safe. Sure there was the thing of him being a woman instead of a man, but he reasoned as badly as she wanted him, she may not care.

But could he really leave his family?

He took a deep breath. "I can't do that."

"Then we don't have a deal. Goodbye, Banks Wales. And good luck."

By T. Styles

Nidia sat in her bedroom with the lights off looking into darkness.

After ending the call with Banks, she started to loathe him deeply. In all of her life, he was the one man who she desired and yet he remained unattainable. Had he not been worth so much to her business, she would have killed him long ago.

Nidia was used to dealing with men who lusted money and power, which she could provide in abundance. And as a result she would bring them closer to their knees. But Banks didn't want frivolous things. He only wanted the end game, which meant being out of coke, and safe with his family on their island.

And so, after suffering yet another *Banks Rejection*, she realized it was time for her to control the narrative. As she did when she was a ten-year-old little girl, who was accosted after being lured to her teacher's home under the pretense of getting candy.

Except there were no treats.

Instead she was passed around by twenty perverted men, with desires of raping a child in mind. At first she cried as pain ripped through her body, but as the days went on, her tears dried up. Besides, no one cared and some got off on her torment. She started to pay attention to what men desired, and once skilled enough, she used their impulses to get them hooked.

Whatever they liked, she did it better.

Before long, in the middle of the night, without the teacher knowing, each man secretly professed their undying love, along with promises to help her escape if she would commit to only them. Of course she lied.

The goal was survival and then escape.

Always.

And when she was thirteen, she used that power to break free with the help of a pedophilic pediatrician.

Within ten minutes of escaping, she called the police and the bad doctor was eventually arrested, along with his sick friends.

All she wanted was to return to the single father who raised her.

And she got her wish.

Back at home, she expected her father to accept her with open arms. But he rejected her, because he was too ashamed to deal with the

260   *By* *T. Styles*

guilt of allowing her to be captured in the first place. Sure he made certain the teacher and the rest of the pedophiles were convicted of their crimes, but he never felt the same about his daughter. There was humiliation looking into her eyes, knowing about all the things she endured.

He felt like a failure.

And still she wanted her father's love.

Things turned dark when relying on what she learned from the perverts, she walked into her father's room one night. Hoping to make him love her again, she slid under the sheet and placed his penis between her lips. Overcome with the amazing way in which she made him tingle, he allowed her to pleasure him until he reached an orgasm.

But the moment she finished, she quickly realized she made a grave mistake. Now fourteen years old, he ordered her to pack her things, took her in his car and dropped her across the border in Mexico. The last thing he wanted was to get locked up, like those he brought to trial, for violating his daughter the same way.

She was alone.

But only for a while.

Her beauty was intoxicating and soon after the younger brother of a Mexican drug boss rescued her from a filthy shelter. Her eyes said she'd seen many things and that was alluring by itself.

Before long their bond grew and he fell deeply in love, but it was Pablo, the drug Lord, who nurtured her until she was old enough to take his bed. And a day after their first sexual experience, when she was eighteen, he made her his wife. Proclaiming there had never been a woman who made him feel *such things* before.

But too many men in her life now damaged Nidia, especially her father. And as a result she could never *love* properly.

She trusted no one. Instead she resorted to her old habits and learned everything about Pablo and his business. And when she had every contact she needed, she slit his throat in their hot tub under the moonlight, met with his business partners the next day, and stole his empire.

A week later she relocated to Texas, where she continued her operation. Her first line of business when her power grew great was to pluck the limbs off her father until he bled to death. She also ordered the painful murders of every man who touched her as a child, whether they were free or in prison.

So what was she to do about Banks Wales?

Whose only crime was loving his family while rejecting her at the same time.

After dialing a number, she waited for the caller to answer. "Mason, is that you?" Nidia asked.

Silence.

She smiled, having felt his shock through the phone. She knew he had been wanting a connection so she was granting his wish.

"Uh, yes, I..."

"I'm sending a plane for you," she continued. "You'll meet with me tonight."

"Indeed."

Three hours later, Mason was sitting in Nidia's dining room, eating cheese and crackers while sipping wine.

Her choice.

There was a silence between them but he was comfortable in it. He refused to make the first move. Besides, he heard tale of her legend and was keen on letting her rule. If he had learned anything from Banks over the years, it was to go with the flow, something he wasn't accustomed to which is why he made many mistakes.

After silence consumed them, finally she said, "I want to discuss business."

He sat his wine glass down and rubbed his hands together. "Okay."

"Upstairs." She nodded toward the ceiling. "In the bedroom."

He was slightly confused, but followed her up the spiral staircase.

Ten minutes later he was lying flat on his back, with her riding his dick. His head was twisted by everything. Was he really fucking the Plug? He couldn't get her on the phone in the past; so never in a million years did he think this would be happening.

Mason was also amazed that although older, she had complete control over the walls of her pussy. Inside she felt like a twenty something year old and he wondered how. Her box seemed to pulsate and stroke his thickness as if she were using slick hands.

Loving the sensation, his fingertips peddled the soft wrinkles of her flesh, which felt like bunches of wrinkled silk. Although much different from Jersey, she was still unique. As he

264   *By T. Styles*

eased in and out of her slippery pussy, he did his best to hold back on reaching an orgasm. In the short time of being in her presence, he believed she felt most powerful in the bedroom, so he let her conduct the meeting.

The moment wasn't about him although it felt like fireworks.

Powerful women were always alluring.

"I'm going to work with you," she said as she rose and fell onto his dick.

He nodded. Hands on her waist, while remaining quiet.

"But, you will need to do everything I say," she continued.

"I'm listening."

"I will give you Banks' territory. But you will give me Banks' head."

He allowed her to outline everything she wanted until she fell into an orgasm on top of his chest. She tried to get up, but he maintained his hold until he bust too. Only then did he let her go.

When they both were done, she slid off of him, while both sat on the edge of the bed.

His silence intrigued her.

She knew he wanted the moment to be on top. So why wasn't he singing her praises?

Mason put on his clothing as she eyed him intently.

When he was done, she broke silence first again. "Your answer?"

He stood up. "No."

She glared. "What you say to me?"

"Banks and I got beef, but it goes deeper than you realize." He paused. "And I ain't about to kill him for you. Whatever I do to him will be based on my plans. You want the nigga dead, you kill him yourself." He moved toward the door.

"It would be a shame to walk out on me."

He looked at her and nodded his head in agreement. "You been hating me all my life. Even when I was a kid." He paused. "Why should that change now?" He bopped out the door readjusting his dick in his jeans.

She was stunned.

She calculated a wrong move.

Sure Mason wanted to get at Banks, after all, he hurt his son. And yes he wanted access to Nidia's cocaine. But to work arm and arm with the enemy, to Mason, felt like a different type of disloyalty. It just wasn't his brand.

By T. Styles

And he wasn't willing to comply. Not even for money.

A few minutes after Mason left, her loyal subjects entered the room. "He's leaving. You want us to bring him back?" One of her men asked.

"No," she smiled.

They were confused at her calm manner.

But Nidia didn't care. She was enlightened for the first time in a long time. Now everything Banks fought for, when he tried to connect her with Mason made sense.

Even though Mason was a Lou, he had a code. And in a world full of savages it was refreshing.

So she let them both go.

In her own way.

For now.

CHAPTER THIRTY-FOUR

B anks was seated in his office.

Time was running out on how he would get his family to safety. The alcohol he was quaffing messed with his mind and as a result, he didn't have his wits about himself.

Still, there was work to be done.

Starting with a phone call he didn't want to make.

Banks dialed a number and took a breath. Seconds later Claire answered. "What do you want?"

"How you holding up?" He asked as if he gave a fuck.

"You may have been friends with my husband but I never liked you," she said truthfully. "I always knew that you would do exactly what you did, ruin our lives."

"I'm sorry." He said honestly.

"Sorry doesn't bring Vanguard back now does it? Sorry doesn't change the fact that my children are without their father."

"You're right."

By T. Styles

"Then please tell me what the fuck you want from me?"

He stood up, walked out of his office and toward the basement. He already had privacy but he needed to move around if he was going to stomach the most racist person alive.

"Are you there!" She yelled from the handset.

Once inside the basement, he closed the door and flopped on the sofa. "I need you, I need you to tell me where Vanguard's plane is located."

"You can't be serious."

"I am. Very serious."

"Nigger, I wouldn't give you a plane if you could shit my husband alive out of your ass! Do not call my number again, or I will file charges!"

When she hung up, Banks tossed the cell across the basement, breaking it into many pieces. He regretted it immediately because it was his only mode of contact.

And for the first time, since Nikki died, tears rolled down his cheek.

Although silent, the pain was no less real as he imagined how once again, those he loved would be ripped away. When the door opened, he stood up and wiped the tears off his face.

Confused and knowing something was wrong, Harris, Joey and Spacey walked inside and up to him.

"Pops, what's wrong?" Harris asked looking at his shattered cell.

"Just get back...get back upstairs."

"No!" Joey said. "We not leaving you!"

"Yeah, Pops," Harris added, "Not this time." He paused. "Now what's wrong? Is it about Minnie?"

"I fucked up, sons," he said shaking his head. "And I put my entire family, everything I love right in the...right in the fucking middle!"

"Pops, I wanted to talk to you about that night, of the shootout," Harris said. "Someone was outside the window and at first I thought he was one of your men but then...everything kicked off."

Banks frowned. "Did you recognize him?"

"No, but I would if I saw him again."

When the door opened, Bet walked inside, interrupting their conversation. Without asking what was happening, she moved toward her husband and gripped him into her arms. Whispering in his ear she apologized for what happened in the bedroom, when in a desperate attempt to feel closer to him, she forgot who he was.

He forgave her.

Seconds later their sons, covered them too.

In that moment, as they embraced, more tears poured down his face, although he never uttered a sound.

Crying in his mind was weak and yet he felt a weird sense of relief.

Tears poured for the loss of his mother.

Tears poured for having killed his own father.

Tears poured for losing Nikki, without giving her the simple life she deserved.

Tears poured for not knowing where Minnie was, and if she was okay.

And tears poured for Mason, for realizing that he would have to kill him dead dead to really save his family.

When he was done, Banks took a deep breath and wiped his eyes. "I'm gonna get us out of this," he promised. "It may take me some more time but we will be on that island."

"Banks, let me help," Bet begged.

"No." Banks said shaking his head.

"Just give me a chance." She paused. "Please. I can do this."

Banks took a deep breath and moved closer. He wanted her to feel his seriousness. "Stay out of it, Bet. I got us."

By T. Styles

CHAPTER THIRTY-FIVE
6:17 AM

Claire poured herself a cup of coffee when there was a knock at the door. She moved into the guesthouse, behind their burned property, which had been blown up earlier that night.

The fire department begged her to stay elsewhere, but since the guesthouse was unharmed she preferred to stay close to her things. And there was nothing they could do to change her mind. Especially since she was out of their way while they investigated the crime.

Banks' men had left immediately after the blow up so there was no more protection. She wouldn't have wanted it anyway. She felt untouchable.

Believing it was another fire or bomb investigator, Claire walked to the door. She was surprised to see a familiar face on the other side.

"May I come in?" Bet asked.

"What is wrong with you people?" She yelled. "Don't you understand the word no?"

Bet pushed her way inside and sat on the sofa, crossing her legs. Nodding her head toward

Claire's coffee cup she asked, "You gonna offer me some?"

Claire closed the door, placed the cup on the table and sat down. "What do you want?"

"Did you get my flowers?"

"What flowers?"

"The ones I sent for your anniversary earlier this year, and every year before that. The only reason I'm asking is because I never got a thank you card."

Claire crossed her arms over her chest. "You know, I never understood why you sent flowers. Unlike my husband, I wanted nothing to do with you. I want nothing to do with you now."

"Because marriage is a powerful unity, when you've found the right person." Bet smiled. "I know what that means because I feel that way for Banks." When Bet's phone rang she looked down at it and sighed when she saw an unrecognizable number.

But she knew who it was.

Using one of his other cells, since he destroyed his main one in the basement, Banks attempted to reach his wife. There was a reason.

He didn't want her anywhere near Vanguard's home.

274

But against Banks' wishes, she decided to meet with Claire anyway, believing she would deal with the consequences later.

Claire sighed. "I'm not giving you my plane." She paused. "From what I hear Banks isn't skilled enough to fly it anyway."

"My husband has twenty years of aviation experience. And the credentials to back it up," Bet paused. "He's respected by the aviation board and can fly almost any aircraft. Now the basics are the same. He can fly that plane I promise you. He's been with Vanguard in it many times."

"I don't care. You won't get ours."

"I will."

She frowned. "What makes you think so?"

"Because you understand what it means to want your family safe. Especially sitting here in a space where you almost lost it all."

"What are you? A sales person?"

Bet smiled. "I spent some time in real estate." She admitted. "You are in a position to help my family, and I need you to do just that."

"Never." She laughed. "I will never help you or your family. Why would I, when you've taken everything from me?"

Bet smiled. "Maybe it was too insensitive for me to come today." Bet stood up. "Here's my number." She handed her a card with her cell. "Call if you change your mind." Before she walked out she said. "By the way, that nigger you speak of had a white mother. Just wanted you to know."

Ten minutes later, Bet was back in her car. When her phone rang again she smiled. Her plan worked, but she knew it would.

"Is it true?" Claire asked. "About his mother?"

Silence.

Claire cleared her throat. "What are you planning to do to me?"

"Excuse me?"

"I think you're threatening me. And my sons. In a passive aggressive way."

"I never said a harsh word."

Claire sighed. "I'm going to give you the location of the plane." She paused. "After that, I want you and your family out of my life."

"Thank you."

After recording the address for the plane in the note app on her phone, she grinned. With one of her troubles over, in that now they could fly to the island, she was slightly relieved. There was still the matter of Minnie but she was certain that Banks would find her, if she would just trust him.

There was one more pressing concern.

She had to visit her parents. That was actually where she told him she was going. And had he known she was going to Claire's instead, he would've never agreed to let her out the house.

But Bet adored her parents. In her eyes, they were the epitome of what love should be. Even now, after many years, Bet saw only what she wanted, ignoring everything else.

Even Banks was clueless on who his parents-in-law were.

He should have dug deeper; because Bet's past would be the key to the darkness coming his way in the near future.

After knocking on the door, when it opened, Bet smiled at her mother who had a blackened eye. To others the bruise would seem majorly out of place but Bet was used to this sort of thing.

And so it didn't bother her at all.

Happy to see her parents, possibly for the last time, Bet hugged her mother and walked inside, locking the door behind herself. "Hey, mama."

"Sweetheart, what happened?" Gerry said. "I'm so confused. There were so many men here and—

"I know, mama." She paused holding her hands. "I was—"

"Bethany!" Before Bet could finish, her father, George, rushed into the room. "Honey, what is going on? It's almost seven o'clock in the morning. And why did Banks send those men over here?"

"Daddy, I'm so sorry," Bet said grabbing his hands, looking up into his eyes. "But I have to tell you both something." They sat on the sofa. "And I don't have a lot of time."

"What is it?" George asked.

"I'm moving."

"Moving?" Gerry said. "But...where...and why?"

"I can't explain a lot right now. Besides, I don't want you in any danger." She paused. "Just know that I have to follow my husband."

"Yes, honey," Gerry said nodding profusely. "Follow your husband wherever you need to go. Even if it means your life."

George frowned. "You saying that now?" He said to Gerry. "But when I asked you to cook lunch yesterday, you said you were tired."

"Mama," Bet yelled. "You never supposed to do that! Is that why you two were fighting?"

278   *By T. Styles*

Gerry looked down in shame.

"After all this time she still doesn't realize what a good man I am," George said glaring at Gerry, wondering if he should hit her again. "I'm starting to think she likes me putting my hands on her."

Bet touched George's hand. "Don't worry, daddy. Eventually mama will understand."

Poor Bet.

After living under a shroud of dysfunction all of her life, she saw only what she wanted. Not because she wasn't concerned for her mother's well being. But by refusing to see her father for who he really was, a monster who did many violent things that would impact Bet immediately if she remembered, she could stay in her fake world.

"So what now?" George asked Bet.

"When I get to where I'm going, I'll reach out," she promised. "I just want you both to know that me and the kids will be safe."

After spending a little more time with them, she hugged them both and climbed into her car. Banks was blowing up her phone so she had to get home quickly, or she would put her marriage in further turmoil.

She was still thinking about her parents when—

WHACK!

Suddenly Bet's car was rocked from the passenger's side by a van and spun out in the middle of the street like a top. Before she could figure out what was happening, her car had crashed into a parked mobile trailer.

In excruciating pain, she was yanked from her vehicle and thrown into a van before it peeled out from the scene.

7:17 AM

Feeling like they were coming down with a cold, Spacey and Joey were in the kitchen making hot toddies. Since Bet was gone, and Banks went to dig up some more cash, in the hopes of buying a new plane from somewhere, they felt they could sip the drink and catch a quick nap afterwards.

Banks had no idea Bet had already secured the aircraft.

By T. Styles

As they sipped their hot toddies, the house phone rang. Spacey's eyes widened when he looked at the caller ID. "What the fuck?"

"Who is it?" Joey asked.

"It's Unc. I think."

"Don't answer."

"What if this about Minnie?" Spacey said. "I got too." Spacey hit the button. "Hello."

"Son, where, where is your father?" Bet wept on the other end.

Upon hearing his mother's voice, Spacey flopped into a chair. He was so scared it was all he could do to hold his bladder.

"What, man?" Joey asked, his heart rocking in his chest while seeing his brother's face.

"It's ma...I think Unc got her." He whispered, covering the mouthpiece.

Seconds later, Mason appeared on the phone. "If you want your mother alive, meet me at Banks' recreation center in Baltimore."

"When?" Spacey asked.

"Now."

CHAPTER THIRTY-SIX
8:14 AM

Lying on Shay's bed, Harris looked up at her pretty face. She had just finished riding his dick and he was already wrecked with guilt.

Why couldn't he leave her alone?

"Why you looking all mad?" She asked, touching his face with her long red designer nails. "I ain't do it right this time either? Because I thought you came when I made my tongue—"

"I hate that they didn't tell us that we were...that we are..."

She was already over the news because her mind was made up. "Then let's charge that to them," Shay continued, lying on top of his chest. "Why should we take on they shit?" She shrugged. "I mean, we already in love and I'm not giving up my nigga."

"Where your pops and mom?" He paused. "You know we leaving soon right? Maybe tonight."

She got off of him, grabbed the sheets and covered her body. "I don't know where they are. They not answering my calls." She paused. "How come I feel like something wrong?"

By **T. Styles**

"Ain't nothing wrong."

"How you know though?" She hoped he'd say the right thing to put her at ease.

"I don't."

"That's honest," she nodded, as she tried to push the bad thought out of her mind. "You heard from Minnie?"

"No, but I'm gonna grab my phone and see if she left a message. I'm the only one she'll call. I just gotta sneak it away from Pops but I don't know where he put our cells when he took 'em. The only reason he connected the house phone was because we all talked in the basement earlier and he wanted to reach us while he was out."

"The floorboard in his office," she said matter of factly. "Check for the cells there."

He frowned. "How you know?"

"I saw him putting something there before so I think it's his favorite hiding space," she paused. "When I knocked on the door looking for daddy one day. You and me had just finished having sex and I was trying to feel him out, to see if he saw us. He didn't. Was too worried about Banks than what we were doing. As usual."

He kissed her cheek, got dressed and snuck toward his father's office.

After the Wales family had a heart to heart earlier, Banks instructed the soldiers to hang outside the mansion instead of inside, to give his family some privacy. Per their request. As a result, none of his men were in the hallways. This meant Harris could move around without their watchful eyes.

Once in Banks' office, after looking around for a while, he eventually found an odd floorboard. He attempted to open it but it didn't budge. He scanned his father's desk and saw an out of place remote. When he hit a button on it the floorboard unlocked. Lifting it up, he saw a bunch of phones, including his, along with some composition books.

"Yes!" He said to himself.

Grabbing his cell, he went past a few voice messages from his friends before stopping on the one Minnie left before she bounced the second time.

"Harris, I know you won't understand what I did to Daddy but he deserved it, when he broke me and Arlyndo up. And for how he knew them crazy bitches kidnapped me and he still let them. He even hurt Natty! Anyway, I just want you to tell the family I'm sorry. But I..." She sniffled. *"I wrote a*

By T. Styles

letter to the FBI, to tell them about the drugs daddy be moving. When they get that letter they'll probably lock him up and send him to a women's prison. He deserves it though. Please forgive me. Bye."

Hearing his little sister was part snitch caused his blood pressure to rise.

What could he do?

He paced Banks' office. Sure they were leaving the country, but if the government learned Banks was a dealer, he was certain they would trace the flight path and tear them up again. He tried to call the number she hit him from, but it went to Hutch's voicemail.

All he knew was this...he had to get that letter.

After going through the closet, he found a wire hanger and extended it. He figured if she mailed the letter earlier, she probably put it in the mailbox some blocks away from the house.

Maybe he could grab it before the mailman picked it up.

So with the stretched hanger in hand, he moved toward the door where he saw one soldier pacing.

Confused Harris approached him. "What's wrong with you?"

"Your brothers left the property," he said hysterically. "And the others went after him." He was so worried he looked like he was about to faint. "I been trying to reach Banks but he won't answer."

Harris scratched his head and remembered Banks broken cell on the floor in the basement. "You won't be able to get him on that one," he paused. "He using another one. I can't remember that number though."

"Fuck!"

"Listen, go to my moms office and look on her desk. I think she got most of his other cell numbers on her planner. Call all of them until he picks up."

"Okay." He nodded. "But whatever you do, stay in the house." He pointed at him. "I can't risk losing somebody else."

The man took off running while Harris ran outside, ignoring everything he said. He had work to do.

Almost half way from the mansion, he located the nearest mailbox. Banks liked the box being

By T. Styles

that far, so that not even a government official would have a reason to come on his property.

8:48 AM

Linden and Tops were sitting in the car yawning and trying to stay up, when they saw Harris walking up the block. Tops was also scrolling through the Gram on his cell.

"You gotta be kidding me," Linden said to himself before looking at Tops. "Ain't that's Banks' son?"

Tops put his cell down. "I guess so. He do look like one of them little red niggas from the dinner shoot out that night."

Curious, they watched him move toward the large blue mailbox, pull open the flap and dig inside with the hanger while shining the flashlight at the same time.

"Fuck he doing?" Tops asked wiping his hand down his scraggly, disconnected beard.

"I don't know, but let's go find out."

When both of them exited the car, they approached Harris from behind, who was still digging into the box with full force.

Sure the plan was stupid. U.S. mailboxes were mostly secure. But the way he saw it was simple. If you didn't live near the property, which nobody else did, there would be no reason to use that mailbox. So he figured Minnie's letter was the only one inside.

If only he could get it.

Right before Linden and Tops were about to snatch the young king, and tuck him in their trunk, a police cruiser pulled up and an officer approached them from behind.

"What are you doing?" The cop asked, as he stepped to the trio who did not see him until he made his presence known.

Harris closed the mailbox and dropped the flashlight and hanger. "Uh...I was..."

"Tampering with federal property," the officer said. Removing his handcuffs from his hip, he slapped them on Harris' wrists. "What's your name boy?"

Silence.

"What's your name?"

By T. Styles

"Harris Kirk Wales." He said proudly.

"Oh really?"

When Linden and Tops tried to walk away, Harris yelled, "Officer, they were helping me break in the box too! They my friends!"

Shocked, Tops and Linden would've taken off running but another officer pulled up on the scene and blocked their car.

"This nigga lying!" Tops yelled.

"Tell that to the judge," an officer replied.

In the end they were all placed under arrest for obstruction of correspondence, which held a $250,000 fine and up to five years in prison.

Tops and Linden were heated to be arrested for something so juvenile.

Ten minutes later, they were sitting in the back of a wagon. Sure Harris could've taken the heat on his own, but he recognized Tops' face from the window the night of the shoot out that destroyed his family's lives.

And linden resembled Mason, so he wanted him gone too.

As many Louisville's Harris could get away from his family the better.

He grinned, all the way to jail.

CHAPTER THIRTY-SEVEN

Banks collected cash from a few secret spots and was headed home when he got a call from one of his frantic soldiers. After Banks listened to the most important detail, that his sons and wife were gone, he felt weak.

It didn't help matters that the soldier was clueless as to where they went. His men were dropping the ball.

All the soldier knew was that Spacey and Joey had been lured from the house. And that they said they were going to help Bet. Who apparently was taken by Mason.

Pulling over, Banks took several deep breaths. He needed a clear mind. "Calm down and listen to what I'm asking. Did they say where they were headed?"

"Uh, uh, I mean...I can't remember."

"THINK HARDER, NIGGA!"

"Oh yeah...something about a rec."

He knew where they were.

Banks hung up, turned his car around and headed toward the airport where his plane once

By *T. Styles*

sat. With his aircraft destroyed, Banks figured he could steal something else.

But the red head was there, at 9:13 in the morning.

He walked up to her and she was still shaken. Makeup had run down her face and she trembled as she placed items into a box.

"Why you here so early on a Sunday?" He asked.

"I thought it would be safe to grab a few of my things. And Banks, I'm so sorry about your plane." She cried. "I didn't know who they were. And there were so many of them."

"Don't worry about that." He touched her hand. "Where you going?"

"I'm taking a leave of absence. I can't deal with...I just can't."

"I understand. But before you go I need a favor."

"I don't have any keys to the planes," she said. "Plus the owner is very upset about those men coming to the—"

"I don't want a plane," he said. "I need something else."

She wiped her tears. "Okay. What is it?"

"You have the keys to PORT A?"

She looked in the direction, toward a large reddish port. "Wait...you want a—"

"Helicopter." He said completing her sentence.

"But...what...I mean..."

"You know I can fly one," he paused "And I promise to leave it somewhere they can find it later."

"But what if they think I gave it to you?" She sniffled. "I could lose my job."

"I'll make them think I took it from you against your will."

"How?"

With that he hit her in the face, knocking her out.

Banks was walking to PORT A when his phone rang. Since it wasn't his regular cell, he wondered outside of his wife and his soldier, who had the number.

Even though time wasn't on his side, he answered anyway. "Hello."

"Banks."

By T. Styles

Banks stopped walking when he heard Mason's voice. "How you get this number?"

"You asking the wrong questions, Blakeslee."

His heart beat harshly in his chest as he heard his birth name. "You got my wife and kids, nigga?"

"Isn't this a great country? Where two bitches can get together in lesbian matrimony?"

"You got my family or not?"

"I told you I'm not playing games with you. You believe me now?"

"You really, really don't wanna do this," Banks said. "I promise you."

"What else can you do to me? Huh? You already took out my best men. Ruined my fucking operation! Blew up my house! What more can happen?"

"I got Derrick."

Silence.

"We really don't wanna go there do we?" He paused. "If a hair on his head is harmed again, every nigga with Wales in their name getting splattered. So—"

"Mason, let my family go. By now you should realize I'm always three steps ahead."

Mason laughed. "Nah, Blakeslee, I'm starting to think you don't realize how many steps ahead *I* am." He paused. "Hurt my son and your whole family dies."

Banks hung up.

He was done talking to the enemy. Besides, there was work to be done. With the keys to the 'Copter, he drove to a house he used to hold a special kind of product.

Explosives.

After losing his cousin in front of his father's house many years ago, Banks had learned all he could obtain about the dangerous weapons. Its power was complete and massive which was why he was seduced by it. He learned that if used correctly, it could get him out of a situation like now. So he taught himself, in secret, how to build and disarm bombs.

And now it was time to use what he learned to his advantage.

Again.

He already showed his skills at Mason's so this was round two.

After getting the special bomb, he went back to the port and pulled out a quiet helicopter. It was a special design that limited noise in cities,

By T. Styles

which were already inundated with sound. So if you didn't know he was coming, you'd be in trouble.

He needed all the help he could get, if he wanted to sneak up on Mason and save his family.

Now in the air, he made a call. "I'm cashing in now," Banks said on the phone.

The caller sighed deeply. "I don't know about this."

"You really wanna be on the wrong side of this war?"

"No."

"Then answer the phone when I hit you back. Give me fifteen minutes."

After landing on top of his recreation center, he turned the engine off and called the man again. He didn't answer. And Banks was forced to call five more times.

He was heated.

After the sixth time, finally he picked up. "Nigga, you playing with me?" Banks asked through clenched teeth.

"No," he whispered. "Mason was around."

"Where is my fucking family?"

"Inside the janitor closet, in the basketball court area."

"Good. I'm leaving a bomb by the back door in the employee's location. I want you to put it where Mason and his soldiers are. Just make sure my family is not where it goes off. It looks like an air filter so it should go unnoticed."

"Won't it go off with me too? If I carry it?"

"Not if you move quickly. It's on a timer."

"Come on, man," Cliff said. "There has to be another way."

"I took care of your family. Got you in Mason's good graces. You thought that shit was for free? It was for this moment right here. Make sure my family safe and put the bomb where Mason and his men are."

"I'll do it when—"

"You'll do it now!"

After hanging up, Banks exited the helicopter and crept toward a door on top of the building. Once inside, he moved toward the control room, which housed all of the machinery necessary to keep the center running. After flipping on the lights inside a small office, he plopped on the edge of a desk and looked at his watch.

By T. Styles

If things went right, the bomb would blow in six minutes.

But when six minutes passed and nothing, he started to believe that he'd done something wrong. Where was the sound? If Cliff didn't bring the explosive in the building, it would still detonate on the side.

Banks felt defeated. Maybe he wasn't as good with explosives as he—

BOOM!

Suddenly the building rocked and the power went out. The security alarms began to sound, which happened after power was disconnected. Crawling out of the control room, he was immediately overtaken by smoke and dust plaster. The thickness moved down his nostrils, making him cough repeatedly. Luckily he knew the area even in darkness so he moved toward the basketball court.

Once inside, his heart dropped when he opened the janitor's door, and didn't see his family. Grabbing a flashlight, he searched the building and didn't find them anywhere.

But there was one place he hadn't checked.

The pool house.

So quickly he moved into that direction.

Once there, slowly he opened the door and was shocked by the hanging debris from the ceiling and more than all the smell.

Chlorine.

Blood.

Those were the odors that permeated Banks' nostrils as he opened the door leading into the large pool house. The moment he was inside, and saw what lie before him, he gasped in disbelief.

Standing near the entrance his breath rose and fell in his chest as he viewed what could only be described as a massacre. Mostly dim, only light from the pool's surface, which was red due to the bloody water, shined against his face in wave like patterns.

Slowly he walked toward the blood bath and down the silver ladder leading into the pool. This would give him nightmares he was certain. The water was crimson thick and was littered with floating limbs that bobbled along like apples in a barrel.

Banks' eyes grew blurry as tears covered his vision. He was forced to deal with what he didn't want to face.

By T. Styles

Did these limbs belong to those he loved? Was he moving past carnage that would later represent losing his entire family?

Again?

Wiping the tears away, he moved through the floating graveyard, picking up body part after part as his mind floated back to when things first got out of hand.

He didn't want to think about the moves he made which contributed to his family's demise. But there was no denying that this was part his fault.

Taking a deep breath he went back to the moment where *once again* he found himself at odds with his most worthy adversary.

His best friend.

Mason Louisville.

After going through the limbs, it became obvious that he couldn't make heads from tails. Too much had happened and he was certain his family was gone.

And then he happened on an arm with a distinct watch on it, which he knew belonged to Mason.

He was dead too.

His mission was accomplished.

But was losing his family worth it?

Although Banks realized Mason's death was necessary if he were to survive, seeing the proof fucked him up in a way he didn't know was possible. In addition to losing his family, he was now rocked with a grief that made him realize what he'd always known.

That he loved his friend.

But they were better foes.

When he heard the sirens in a distance, he crawled out of the pool and made it outside without being seen. His world felt like it was over.

His bomb plan was stupid and dangerous and he felt ill.

The Wales family was no more.

Overcome with grief, he wondered what would have happened if he was successful in killing himself as a little girl. Maybe he wouldn't have brought kids into the world and Bet would be alive.

All he had was a bunch of maybes that would do nothing for him in the moment. But they kept him company as he contemplated dark moves.

And just as his thoughts grew bleak, a black van pulled up alongside him. Too devastated to be afraid or scared that it was an ambush, he looked

By T. Styles

over, only to see Cliff in the driver's seat and Bet in the passenger's seat. Her face was scratched up from when they snatched her out of the car but for the most part, she was free.

She jumped out of the car, ran up to him and cried in his arms. Seconds later Joey and Spacey rushed out and gripped him too. Banks was stunned still, unable to move due to the extreme relief.

They were all alive!

Standing in the middle of the street, the three of them hugged tightly while being overjoyed that everyone was safe.

Separating from their embrace, Banks looked at them each. "Are you hurt?"

"We're good, dad." Spacey said.

He looked at Bet's face.

"I'm fine," she said before he could ask.

Banks nodded. "Okay, okay..." Something was wrong. "Wait, where's Harris?"

Bet sighed. "He got locked up."

Banks felt gut punched. The news wasn't even an option. For one, when was their time to get in trouble with the law? "For what?" He yelled.

"Something about tampering with a mailbox." Bet looked down. "And Mason's brother is with him too. I'm afraid, Banks."

Banks frowned. This was the worse case scenario. "I'm gonna get him out." He nodded. "Don't worry." He kissed her again. "Trust me."

"But, Banks, Claire gave us the plane," she said excitedly.

His eyes widened.

"She said no." He reminded her.

"She changed her mind! She changed her mind, Banks!"

"Well I'm getting you all out today." He kissed her lips. "Get in the van. We need to move now."

As they piled inside, Banks walked over to Cliff and shook his hand. "What happened? How you get them out?"

"Mason was acting strange toward them," Cliff said. "I didn't like how he looked so when he left the room to do something, I freed them and then told them to go out back and wait for me. Until I put the bomb in place."

"What about Mason?" He already knew the answer but he wanted to know for sure. "Was he in the building?"

By T. Styles

"Yes," he paused. "He dead. For sure. He was in the pool house when I dropped the bomb off. I saw him talking to his niggas and everything."

Banks remembered the limb with the watch.

"What now, Pops?" Spacey asked from the window.

Banks was still stunned.

"Like I said I'm getting you away. And then I'm coming back for Minnie and Harris."

It was a long flight.

Almost eight hours.

But in the end the Wales family had made it to the island.

When Banks landed the plane, and his family poured out, they were overwhelmed with its allure. Colors were richer than anything that they ever imagined. The sand was the hue of gold and the water was so blue it looked enhanced. There was even a smooth breeze that rolled lightly upon the island, which caused the luscious green palm trees to dance in their honor.

And then there was the Wales Mansion.

It was glorious.

Banks himself had seen it before and even he stood in awe of the design he created. It resembled a castle with modern flare with its cream structure and colorful cathedral windows.

Everything sparkled.

"Banks," Bet cried, covering her mouth. "You built this for us?"

He kissed her cheek.

"Wow, Pops," Spacey said. "This...this really ours? The whole island?"

Banks nodded.

Joey's eyes widened. "It almost looks like...like..."

"Heaven," the family said completing Joey's sentence.

Walking inside their new home, everything smelled new because it was.

And after meeting with the staff who had vowed to care for them, they realized they were a perfect match. Referring to them as Mr. Wales and Mrs. Wales respectfully, The Valdez family was so happy to meet their new bosses that a few of them cried.

By T. Styles

Both Joey and Spacey also had to catch their breath when they saw two of the four daughters who would be helping care for their land and property. With both families being in complete isolation, they were certain that they would be forced to make the beautiful women their wives. Which is another reason Banks selected that particular family.

He had thought of everything.

There was even a son for Minnie.

As the Wales prince's searched their mansion, and checked out their rooms, Bet walked over to her husband.

"Now all you have to do is find our daughter and get Harris out of jail." Bet said looking up at him. "Then all of this will be complete."

He touched her face. "I'm bringing them back." He said. "Trust me."

When his phone rang he frowned, removed it from his pocket and looked at the screen.

"Who is that?" Bet asked.

"I don't know. Nobody has this number." It rung again. "Go check on the kids."

When she walked away he answered.

It was Nidia.

"So you're a woman," she laughed. "It all makes sense now."

His heart dropped.

With everything going on between Mason and himself, he never thought he would reveal his secret. He didn't know the secret had gotten out earlier, because he was focused and no one told him. Had he known the city knew he would've died from embarrassment long ago.

The hurt was crippling and he began to hate Mason to the next level.

And if he were alive, he'd kill him all over again.

By T. Styles

CHAPTER THIRTY-EIGHT
FCI LOW - DORM ROOM
PRESENT DAY - CHRISTMAS EVE

K irk looked amongst all of the men who were so glued onto his every word, they couldn't catch their breaths. A natural storyteller, they were sad to see the tale come to an end.

By now, as they glanced down at Linden it had become painfully obvious that he was dead.

So the ending was somewhat poetic.

What also happened, that the men weren't aware of, is a second group of inmates, as the story was being told, covered them.

By listening to Kirk, they had let their guards down. Big mistake.

"So the story ends with you getting locked up?" Byrd asked, his missing tooth made his words whistle. The bloody tissue from his busted mouth on the floor below. The crumbled heap held his tooth also.

Kirk glared.

"We want more," Clay said.

"So what you gonna do now?" Byrd asked Kirk. "Cause you may have been a boss on the street, but in here you just another nigga." He rubbed his crusty hands together. "And we not taking the rap for you for killing this dude."

"Exactly," Clay said. "You want us to stay quiet 'bout this here," He pointed at Linden, "Then you gotta grease palms."

"Watch out, young niggas," Tops said standing up. "You still talking to a king."

Suddenly the outer group of men moved in closer and within seconds, calloused palms slammed down over the men's lips as they were jabbed multiple times in the back. By the time the carnage was over, eight trained killers with dripping blood-covered shanks in their hands surrounded Tops, Byrd and Clay.

The surviving three.

They were so shocked that they were too afraid to move. Plus the massacre happened that quickly.

Tops, Byrd and Clay looked back at the men and then Kirk.

"So you gonna kill us too?" Tops said. "I could've blew up your spot the moment we got locked up together," he paused. "Especially since you lied that we helped you break into that mailbox." He pointed at him. "But I didn't."

By T. Styles

Kirk smiled. "I lied on you for a reason."

"And what's that?" He asked through clenched teeth.

"To kill you." He paused. "For starting this war. I saw you fire in our window. At first I wasn't sure who you were but now I know you were with the Lou's. And I don't want you around me or my family."

Byrd and Clay looked behind them at the men, but realized they couldn't run. Instead they were grabbed...two killers on Clay and Byrd and Four on Tops.

"Come on, man," Byrd begged. "Don't hurt me."

"Yeah, Kirk, you ain't gotta do this," Clay added.

"Before I told my story I asked if you were sure you wanted to hear the rest. Each of you said yes. Now you know the reason for my question."

Byrd was shanked quickly and lost his fight. Clay soon followed and entered the afterlife. Tops gave a good try, but in the end his enormous body hit the floor like the rest, as blood gushed from his wounds.

Standing amongst dead inmates, Kirk took a deep breath and looked at his men.

He smiled.

It was perfect.

The moment Banks discovered where his son was being held, he made moves. Moves that not only would protect Harris but also would ensure he would join his family on Wales Island.

By Christmas.

"Why you hit Linden early?" Kirk asked Zion. "I paid for next week."

"You ain't hear?" He responded. "Linden was getting out on bail tomorrow."

"Nah, I ain't know 'bout that." Kirk smiled. "Good looking out though."

Zion grinned. "No doubt."

"You know what you have to do now." Kirk paused. "No major organs." He raised his arms.

Zion looked at the men behind him and back at Kirk. They all shook their heads no, wanting no part of the gruesome chore.

"You sure about this, man?" He paused. "I don't want Banks mad at me."

"This his idea," he paused. "It's part of the plan." He continued. "Now hit me."

Pulling out a fresh shank, within seconds Kirk lie on the floor, amongst the others, bleeding from the gut. In more pain than he thought was

By T. Styles

possible he whispered, "Go sound the alarm." He paused. "Quick!"

EPILOGUE

There was an outsider in the midst.

After Banks piloted most of his family safely to Wales Island, and walked inside the mansion, Mason crawled out of the floorboard from the storage area of the plane, covered in vomit, feces and urine. Having been below deck for eight hours, he was exhausted and eager to breathe fresh air.

Walking toward a group of palm trees, he gazed at the property and breathed deeply. Within seconds his life long asthma issue went away.

He had known Banks all of his life and couldn't help but feel proud at what he built. Mason also realized he didn't think far enough for himself and his family, and that he would have to expand his horizons for the future.

But first things first.

"You did good, Banks," Mason said to himself, taking in the island and all its eminence. "Real good."

With Banks' mind scattered before the flight, he didn't realize that Mason was smarter than he gave him credit for. Mason knew there was

By T. Styles

nothing that would keep Banks from getting his family to the island, so he did a few things himself.

First he had Whoyawanmetabe place a bomb in Vanguard's house. Then he made sure that Vanguard's phone was bugged in the main house and the guesthouse too, so that when Claire spoke on the phone, or even talked around the device, he would hear the conversation in detail.

And that's what happened.

Within a matter of hours, when Claire went off on Banks for Vanguard's murder, only to call back and give Bet the location to the plane later, Whoyawanmetabe and Mason recorded it all.

Having the information in his pocket was only part of Mason's plan. He needed to create a rouse so he could get on that aircraft. So after kidnapping Bet, he led his sons to the rec too.

He even cut off Garret's arm after he killed him, and placed his watch on his wrist. Knowing that Banks would believe he was dead.

Of course he had no idea that Banks would blow his soldiers up to get the Wales clan out of the rec. But what he did know was that he would come in with heavy firepower to save the lives of those he loved.

In fact he was banking on it.

How else could he reach the plane before Banks without a distraction?

Sure he could've murdered his family. But Mason knew that Banks had dealt with great loss before and was immune. After all, he killed his own father and came back. Mason reasoned that if he murdered Banks' family, although Banks would've been sad, Mason felt he would later retreat to Wales Island after he grieved, virtually living in paradise for the rest of his life.

Nah.

If he was going to rock Banks' world he had to touch everything he loved, *especially* the island. So after leading his own men to the pool house, sacrificing their lives in the process, Mason hit it to Vanguard's plane. Hiding inside his air controlled storage area.

The flight was rough. He vomited repeatedly and felt like he would die. But hate kept him alive.

And now he had arrived.

Undetected.

Removing his phone from his pocket he called Howard. "You got him yet?"

"Yeah, he here. Fucked up too."

By T. Styles

"How you get him out of Banks' house?"

"Wasn't nobody there like you said. So we pulled him out one of the rooms we be staying in when we used to spend the night. He was bleeding bad though."

Mason's jaw twitched. "How bad?"

"Just his toe," he paused. "It's gone. He sleeping now. Ma gave him some pain medicine and the Doc came by complaining as usual."

He sighed. "What about your mother? How is she?"

"Better that Derrick here. She with her brother now."

Mason frowned. "Her brother? Your mother ain't got no family outside of us."

"That's what I thought."

Confused he said, "Put her on the phone."

"She don't wanna talk right now."

Mason shook his head. "Listen, I don't want you mad at her. For drugging you. She did what she knew how to make sure you and your brothers were safe."

"I'm over it," Howard sighed. "I'm still mad at you though. For hitting her the way you did." He paused. "But we'll talk about all that later. So what now?"

Mason took a deep breath and looked at the beautiful island again. "I found our paradise." He eyed Banks' land with envy.

"For real?"

"Yep. Got a name for it and everything. I'm calling it The Land Of The Lous. Wait 'till you see this shit."

By T. Styles

COMING SOON

WAR 3:
THE LAND OF THE LOUS

CARTEL PUBLICATIONS

P R E S E N T S

The Cartel Publications Order Form

www.thecartelpublications.com
Inmates **ONLY** receive novels for $10.00 per book **PLUS** shipping fee **PER BOOK.**
(Mail Order **MUST** come from inmate directly to receive discount)

Shyt List 1	_____	$15.00
Shyt List 2	_____	$15.00
Shyt List 3	_____	$15.00
Shyt List 4	_____	$15.00
Shyt List 5	_____	$15.00
Pitbulls In A Skirt	_____	$15.00
Pitbulls In A Skirt 2	_____	$15.00
Pitbulls In A Skirt 3	_____	$15.00
Pitbulls In A Skirt 4	_____	$15.00
Pitbulls In A Skirt 5	_____	$15.00
Victoria's Secret	_____	$15.00
Poison 1	_____	$15.00
Poison 2	_____	$15.00
Hell Razor Honeys	_____	$15.00
Hell Razor Honeys 2	_____	$15.00
A Hustler's Son	_____	$15.00
A Hustler's Son 2	_____	$15.00
Black and Ugly	_____	$15.00
Black and Ugly As Ever	_____	$15.00
Ms Wayne & The Queens of DC **(LGBT)**	_____	$15.00
Black And The Ugliest	_____	$15.00
Year Of The Crackmom	_____	$15.00
Deadheads	_____	$15.00
The Face That Launched A	_____	$15.00
Thousand Bullets		
The Unusual Suspects	_____	$15.00
Paid In Blood	_____	$15.00
Raunchy	_____	$15.00
Raunchy 2	_____	$15.00
Raunchy 3	_____	$15.00
Mad Maxxx (4th Book Raunchy Series)	_____	$15.00
Quita's Dayscare Center	_____	$15.00
Quita's Dayscare Center 2	_____	$15.00
Pretty Kings	_____	$15.00
Pretty Kings 2	_____	$15.00
Pretty Kings 3	_____	$15.00
Pretty Kings 4	_____	$15.00
Silence Of The Nine	_____	$15.00
Silence Of The Nine 2	_____	$15.00
Silence Of The Nine 3	_____	$15.00
Prison Throne	_____	$15.00

By T. Styles

Drunk & Hot Girls _____	$15.00
Hersband Material **(LGBT)** _____	$15.00
The End: How To Write A _____	$15.00
Bestselling Novel In 30 Days (Non-Fiction Guide)	
Upscale Kittens _____	$15.00
Wake & Bake Boys _____	$15.00
Young & Dumb _____	$15.00
Young & Dumb 2: Vyce's Getback _____	$15.00
Tranny 911 **(LGBT)** _____	$15.00
Tranny 911: Dixie's Rise **(LGBT)** _____	$15.00
First Comes Love, Then Comes Murder _____	$15.00
Luxury Tax _____	$15.00
The Lying King _____	$15.00
Crazy Kind Of Love _____	$15.00
Goon _____	$15.00
And They Call Me God _____	$15.00
The Ungrateful Bastards _____	$15.00
Lipstick Dom **(LGBT)** _____	$15.00
A School of Dolls **(LGBT)** _____	$15.00
Hoetic Justice _____	$15.00
KALI: Raunchy Relived _____	$15.00
(5th Book in Raunchy Series)	
Skeezers _____	$15.00
Skeezers 2 _____	$15.00
You Kissed Me, Now I Own You _____	$15.00
Nefarious _____	$15.00
Redbone 3: The Rise of The Fold _____	$15.00
The Fold (4th Redbone Book) _____	$15.00
Clown Niggas _____	$15.00
The One You Shouldn't Trust _____	
The WHORE The Wind	
Blew My Way _____	$15.00
She Brings The Worst Kind _____	$15.00
The House That Crack Built _____	$15.00
The House That Crack Built 2 _____	$15.00
The House That Crack Built 3 _____	$15.00
The House That Crack Built 4 _____	$15.00
Level Up **(LGBT)** _____	$15.00
Villains: It's Savage Season _____	$15.00
Gay For My Bae _____	$15.00
War _____	$15.00
War 2: All Hell Breaks Loose _____	$15.00

(**Redbone 1 & 2** are **NOT** Cartel Publications novels and if **ordered** the cost is **FULL** price of $15.00 **each**. **No Exceptions**.)

Please add **$5.00** for shipping and handling fees for up to **(2) BOOKS PER ORDER**.

Inmates too!

The Cartel Publications * P.O. BOX 486 OWINGS MILLS MD 21117

(See Next Page for ORDER DETAILS)

WAR 2: ALL HELL BREAKS LOOSE 319

Name: _____

Address: _____

City/State: _____

Contact/Email: _____

Please allow **8-10 BUSINESS** *days* **before** *shipping.*

The Cartel Publications is <u>NOT</u> responsible for <u>Prison Orders</u> rejected!

<u>*NO RETURNS and NO REFUNDS*</u>
<u>*NO PERSONAL CHECKS ACCEPTED*</u>
<u>*STAMPS NO LONGER ACCEPTED*</u>

320   *By T. Styles*

CPSIA information can be obtained
at www.ICGtesting.com
Printed in the USA
LVHW111437310119
605945LV00001B/139/P